THE FIENDS
IN THE FURROWS

An Anthology of Folk Horror

THE
FIENDS
IN THE
FURROWS

An Anthology of Folk Horror

Edited by
DAVID T. NEAL & CHRISTINE M. SCOTT

N✦P

NOSETOUCH PRESS

CHICAGO | PITTSBURGH

For Bombini

CONTENTS

INTRODUCTION

What is Folk Horror? At its heart, this highly subjective sub-genre of Horror is weird fiction firmly rooted in European pagan tradition—with superstition, folklore, belief, and modernity clashing in ill-omened and menacing ways.

Historically, it has been exemplified in literature in the works of British writers such as M.R. James, Arthur Machen, Algernon Blackwood, Susan Cooper, and Robert Aickman, who successfully captured the persistent eeriness of English landscapes and the essence of ambiguity and occult unease, presented in ancient pagan imagery and motifs grafted to the paranoia of modern life.

Onscreen, Folk Horror's unholy trinity remains *The Witch-finder General* (1968), *The Blood on Satan's Claw* (1971), and the canonical *The Wicker Man* (1973)—these movies eerily harnessed a spirit of their time, during a time of exemplary British Horror films. They continue to cast a long shadow in framing popular perceptions of both the possibilities and limitations of Folk Horror.

Other movies, such as *The Children of the Corn* (1984), *The Blair Witch Project* (1999) and, more recently, *Kill List* (2011), *The Witch* (2015), and *The Ritual* (2017) have picked up some of the uncanny elements that were present in those earlier films, some with an American setting and spin, and with strikingly memorable, sometimes iconic visions of Folk Horror.

The Fiends in the Furrows: An Anthology of Folk Horror attempts to bring more attention to the literary aspects of Folk Horror, both as an homage to its origins, as well as exploring less-traveled paths that might point toward new directions for it, as it continues to develop.

In this collection of nine short stories, you'll find Coy Hall's haunting "Sire of the Hatchet" following a pair of hapless souls attempting to carry out their dreadful mission in a frightfully insular community.

Sam Hicks delivers readers "Back Along the Old Track" into a brooding, multi-generational horror, while Lindsay King-Miller's "The Fruit" stretches Folk Horror into the fecund fields of a monstrous orchard. Steve Toase hurls the reader into "The Jaws of Ouroboros" and a nightmare landscape of ravenous megaliths.

Eric J. Guignard's disarmingly folksy "The First Order of Whaleyville's Divine Basilisk Handlers" serves up the first of several scaled menaces that slithered their way into our anthology, and a theme that organically arose around snake handling.

Romey Petite's unforgettable "Pumpkin, Dear" pursues a doomed farm couple through the growing seasons and back again, while Stephanie Ellis brings "The Way of the Mother" into a more classically Folk Horror posture, in a land of ghastly rituals and all-powerful god-monsters.

Zachary Von Houser's "Leave the Night" carries its protagonist into a deeply traditional Folk Horror nightmare, as a whiskey-addled protagonist keen to escape the city soon finds himself in over his head. Finally, S.T. Gibson's "Revival" finds that old time religion venomously snaking its way back, to the peril of those who would dare to dance with vipers and tempt Fate, itself.

Nosetouch Press is proud to feature these writers, and we hope that Horror fans who are looking for both traditional

Folk Horror tales as well as ones that seek to clear and till new ground for it find these stories to be as horrifying and entertaining as we did.

We're looking forward to seeing how Folk Horror continues to grow and evolve as an offshoot of Horror, and hope *The Fiends in the Furrows* helps plant those sinister seeds where they can thrive.

You reap what you sow,

David T. Neal

COY HALL

SIRE OF THE HATCHET

It looked more like a child. The mound drew him. Hutter stopped in the road so suddenly that his companion walked ten paces before noticing. The companion, too, then stopped and turned, but his eyes were glazed and tired rather than curious. He reminded Hutter of the hour, of their destination. His face was drawn and pinched, vitriolic.

"Something crawled from the hillock," Hutter whispered, cautious of his voice in the surrounding forest. It dawned on him that neither he nor his assistant had spoken in several hours. The road seemed nothing more than a vein in a vast body here, hidden once but now teased to the fore and blue. Was it days of travel that infected him? *You're seeing things*, he thought.

"Codswallop," the companion, a rogue named Wolfric, said.

Hutter placed his satchel on the dirt. He drew the hatchet from the twine at his waist and gripped a handle laced with carvings. He moved into the shadow of the overhanging trees. It was summer and the canopy was thick. The cool wind from the tree line felt anything but pleasant, however. The forest was alive with the chatter of insects and the stench of rotten vegetation.

Wolfric, a nervous man without provocation, was at his side now, a dagger longer than his hand in his grip. "A highwayman?" he asked. God knows he'd feared such a happening for the entirety of the journey. As the companion of an executioner, Wolfric had a head full of stories. If there were a time when he believed all men were human, it had been before he made the acquaintance of Hutter. And with executioners, there was always the specter of revenge.

"It looked more like a child," Hutter said.

"You need an axe for a child?" Wolfric, mercurial, now laughed.

"It *looked* like a child."

"Why don't we get on, then?"

Hutter found himself being honest. "I don't know," he admitted. After all, the mound drew him. There was something magnetic in its pulse. With that, he stepped through a ditch and moved towards the mound. Wolfric remained on the road. Hutter mashed dead leaves, causing a racket. He stood out, a lumbering oaf with a blade, but he couldn't help himself. The mound looked too small, too well shaped, to be natural. It stood only ten feet from the floor of the forest. If man-made, he surmised, thinking of his home in Saxony where there were similar mounds, then this was what his father called one of the old fairy doors. The ancestors of man, heathens of filth, erected mounds to worship devils. His father, a member of the Pietist sect of the Lutheran faith, was colorful in his hatred for pagans. *Ours is a curious heritage,* Hutter thought, stepping still closer. *We reject it and admire it.* From what he had heard on the coast, Indians across the sea built mounds, too. *Cathedrals of filth*, he thought, *but everyone wants to see them.*

What had he seen crawl from the knoll? Was it more than a shadow show? A feeling with depth, akin to dread, spread inside. Now so close to the mound, he faced the real question. Could a tangle of roots scuttle forth like an infant?

Hutter circled the mound, hatchet at the ready, but found nothing but leaves and lances of sunlight. Gnats swarmed his head every moment he stopped. He circled twice, but was cautious not to touch, let alone climb, the mound. The only smell was that of raw earth, pleasing rather than threatening.

Wolfric stood on the road in sunlight, cupping his hand against his mouth, shouting things about the hour.

A fetus of roots, Hutter thought. *An abomination.* God, how it appeared so clearly in his mind. "It's nothing," he called out. "Branches," he said. "Shadows." The words stuck in his throat. Hutter made his way again, still gripping the hatchet, toward the road, the only thoroughfare to the village of his calling. His destination was a hamlet of the English called Strattonwick. His duty was that of an executioner.

Suffering is holy. Strattonwick hung like a broken jaw above the generous floodplain, disjointed and cockeyed, almost strewn across two hillsides. The village possessed the symmetry of an unexpected heave, of something spewed. This was one of the old communal villages, everything shared by the inhabitants and everything owned by the local Earl. The people were more like employees than inhabitants of the estate. The plain abutted the branch of a dark river, and vegetables grew plentiful in the field's rich soil. Men with beaten utensils moved between the rows, swatting insects that preyed on their sweat. A single road skirted the gardens, winding up the hillside on one end and disappearing into a forest on the other. The road was empty of traffic save for two bedraggled strangers on foot. The sun was nearly down, so shadows moved in the branches, deepening. The moon was faintly visible in the sky. Mosquitos and bats swarmed the slow-moving river. It was rumored in Strattonwick that a single wolf had somehow found its way into the forest again. Sometimes men listened for the predator, but it was never seen. The men in the gardens did see the travelers, and they stopped their work, standing erect and staring.

Wolfric sneered at Hutter. How he hated his fellow man. Hutter adjusted his satchel and kept his pace. Instinctively, he touched the hatchet at his waist. He understood men like this, petty and defensive folk who talked honor and dishonor while grubbing in the earth, and who watched all strangers like they were wolves in a nursery. "Chin up," he told Wolfric. "We'll be leaving the richer."

"I'd like to smash them all with the back end of an axe." His face went red as blood, and the veins of hard drinking emerged along his nose.

Hutter shook his head. Unlike Wolfric, he accepted his place in the world. Maybe it was because his father, too, had been an executioner. As a boy, he'd learned how men treated those in the dishonorable trades. His own sons would face the same looks one day. Wolfric claimed higher descent, though this was dubious. His family, too, was scum, his father a mercenary.

Three men emerged from the gardens and walked to the road. Each of the men held a hoe as if it were a cudgel, and each tried to ignore the insects at their shoulders. Occasionally, a hand went up in defense, but it was an act begrudged. Hutter stopped Wolfric, observing a custom he'd learned as a journeyman. From his satchel, he retrieved the papers that identified him as a master in the trade. The men, though they certainly could not read, would demand to see papers. Then they would make a show of letting their eyes linger, full of consternation, on what appeared to be meaningless curls and tangles. Custom transcended education.

When the two groups met at the base of an incline, all was silent save for the chorus of frogs on the shore and the drone of insects in the woods. The men smelled of oxen feces. "We're here for the girl," Hutter said. He offered the papers, pressed with the signature of his father, the man to whom, so many years ago, he'd apprenticed.

There was not an elder among the workers. All three of the men were youthful, the age of new fathers. The man who'd accepted the papers stepped closer, separating himself. He had a dirt-scarred face and a bulbous nose. He was balding, save for a shock of blond hair at the crown of his head. He spoke with the gait of an imbecile. He was not one to be mocked, though. He was thick in the shoulders and possessed hands like granite. He looked like he could tear a man's arm out by the roots. "They're waiting," he said. "You go ask for Master Croft. You show him this."

Hutter took back the papers and nodded. The men turned towards the field, and they whispered to one another. *Sentinels*, he thought.

"And that's the best of them," Wolfric said. "The spokesman."

"I notice you waited till he was gone to say that."

"I'm only a fool when I drink," he said.

Hutter and Wolfric walked up the hillside. This branch of the forest road ended with a smattering of thatched-roof hovels and stone chimneys. Women and children and old men moved about the structures and a series of roiling cauldrons. Oxen moved about with relative freedom, like pet dogs. A fenced sty kept pigs at bay. The only building with any multigenerational permanence was the Strattonwick church house, built with cut planks and fortified with river stones. Still, even this structure was barren, lacking ornamentation. The church was squat and grey and sturdy, and it stood beside a stall of milking cows.

An elder waited at the door of the church, looking pensive. Despite the evening heat, he wore the heavy brown coat of a Puritan. Beneath his hat, his grey hair was cut like a bowl, another mark of his inclination. He was an austere man, judging by the look on his face. He glanced up, revealing a grizzled visage, scarred by a sword thrust at his cheek. One of his hands was missing, and the skin at his wrist was slick and shining. He was once a soldier, Hutter surmised.

"We're looking for Master Croft," Hutter said. Wolfric, tense, stood silently at his side.

"I'm Croft," the old man said. He reached out and accepted the papers offered. With a succinct, educated manner, he scanned the document. He covered Hutter and Wolfric with a quick look, too, stopping a moment on the exposed hatchet at Hutter's waist and the dagger at Wolfric's. "Very well," he said. "Master Hutter, welcome. And your companion?"

"Wolfric Blum, my assistant."

"Master Blum," Croft said. "I'm Israel Croft, the pastor here in Strattonwick. The schoolteacher and magistrate for Lord Allingham, likewise. This is my mission," he said, almost defensively. Then he drank in the smoky, putrid air of the village. Godly intentions, he seemed to say, were nothing to be embarrassed about.

"Suffering is holy," Wolfric observed.

Israel Croft could send a man to hell with his glance, and he let it linger on Wolfric.

Jesus, Hutter thought. Croft was fire and brimstone.

"Come into the church," Croft finally said. "You can sleep here, but nowhere else. I cannot invite you to my home, you understand. It would be dishonorable. It wouldn't be proper. And there's no inn."

"Indeed, it wouldn't," Hutter said. He did his best to pretend the rebuke had no impact.

The three men walked into the open church. It was musty and hot, dark from a lack of windows.

"I'll introduce you to the quarry in the morning," Croft said. "We'll pay you to interrogate her. Then, of course, we'll pay for what follows."

"That's understood," Hutter said.

With that, Croft began showing the executioners around his meager church. When it was too dark to see, he lit a precious candle and extended the flame with his quivering hand. He promised to pray for their souls. That, too, would be part of their pay. He offered the men the "Harlot Pews" at the back of the church for sleeping. He personally brought the executioners two bowls of gruel when the night was full.

I saw it, too. In the complete darkness of the church, stretched on the hard, wooden pews, Hutter tried to sleep, but his mind kept wandering to the mound he'd spied earlier in the day. He turned from shoulder to shoulder, rustling the blanket draped across his legs. Fear, of which he was not proud, grew in his heart. He thought of his own sons, boys who complained of things in the dark. *Shameful,* he thought, *for a man to feel this way.*

Wolfric, in the pew directly ahead, stirred, too. His voice, when it came out of the darkness, was not unwelcome. From what he asked, it was clear he, too, was thinking of the mound.

"What'd you see today?" he asked. The two men had not spoken for hours, and now this.

Hutter turned the question over in his mind. "You're wanting honesty."

"I am." Wolfric had to be deep in thought to be so solemn. Something ate at him.

The image had not left Hutter's thoughts. He knew it well. "Tree roots shaped like an infant, like bones arranged in a skeleton. It moved from the mound."

"It crawled, didn't it?" Wolfric asked.

"It crawled out of the mound. I saw it no more, though."

Wolfric breathed deeply. For several minutes, he said nothing. Wind, the front of a budding thunderstorm, moved through the plank walls, trembling the wood and whistling through stone. The change of air made the cows outside the wall stir and complain. Hutter was prepared to let the matter drop, and to try for sleep again.

"I saw it, too," Wolfric said.

This was not the stability Hutter had sought when answering the question. He wanted to be rebuked for his childishness. He had no desire for affirmation. "On the mound?" The wind became something physical in his mind then and he started with every sigh the storm caused in the darkness.

"After. It was following us along the road, crawling in the trees."

"Watching us? Why?" Hutter had been careful not to touch the mound, and he said as much.

Wolfric did not offer an answer. Neither he nor Hutter dared say what was on their mind.

She drowned the child in earth. "Witchcraft," Israel Croft said. "Witches are the Devil's soldiers, and this girl is no less." The Puritan led the executioners through Strattonwick. He was no stranger to having a captive audience, and he treated Hutter and Wolfric as such. He couldn't help but to preach, even in response to simple questions. He prattled on about witches.

The villagers were up with the morning sun, surveying the damage of a quick thunderstorm that had rushed through prior to dawn. The sky was clear now and the air was muggy, thick. Birds made racket as they flew down to the river. When the executioners passed, the villagers looked away, lest they be tainted. It was a ritual these people had learned from their parents. The gesture, in their minds at least, somehow inoculated them against dishonor. Not even poor folk, not even the rogues who hauled human shit to the gardens or carried squawking chickens by their feet to the slaughter, felt akin to Hutter and Wolfric. They were as good as outlaws. No one bothered to greet the men who had arrived with the sole intention of doing Strattonwick's dirty work.

Croft went on. "I've no doubt Rosamond dabbled in such things. She was no woman of the church. No one ever called her goodwife by mistake." At this, he chuckled. It was a dry, ugly laugh. "She was a heathen of the forest."

"I loathe Puritans," Wolfric muttered. And it was no empty remark. He'd had run-ins with their kind, even in Saxony. He found them joyless hypocrites.

Croft rubbed his face with the nub of his left wrist, a motion that probably appeared as unnatural and frightening as a scarecrow to children. He was such a thin wraith of a man. "Witchcraft is not the reason you're here, as you know." The comment had the ring of disappointment. "Rosamond murdered her child when it was but a newborn." He stopped and turned. "That much you know. There's more to it. She drowned the child in earth," he said. The preacher paused, allowing the gravity of this to sink in.

Hutter found the idea repulsive. It was, in his mind, the worst of the crimes he encountered. The perpetrator was worthy of a hard death. He thought of his own sons and wife. He couldn't fathom the depth of such an act. He grimaced.

"She stuffed dirt in the boy's mouth until he choked. She clamped his mouth with the palm of her hand. Drowned in his own body." Croft's eyes widened. "Then she buried him in the woods. Thank God one of the local girls saw her. No one ever even knew Rosamond was pregnant. She showed no signs. Satan can manipulate what we see, though. Then again, she came and went. I believe the heathen begged on the forest road. Probably sold her flesh."

Rattled, Hutter asked, "She hasn't confessed?"

"The threat of Hell didn't sway her," Croft admitted. "We're hoping your tools will. Of course, with a witness, a confession isn't fully necessary. The drowning will go on tomorrow, regardless. But a confession would make things cleaner for the Earl, Lord Allingham. What with a young girl being the witness. Women lie, as you're no doubt aware. Products of weak Eve. I'd like you to work her over today, see what you can extract."

"We'd like to see her," Hutter said.

"We'll start now," Wolfric added.

Croft nodded.

A rudely constructed shed, built from scrap, roofed with insect-ridden thatch, housed Rosamond. At the rear of the village, on an incline where the hill started upward again, the shed was largely removed from the daily bustle. The forest loomed over the structure, casting shadows. The surrounding weeds were thick with dew. Normally, the shed housed garden tools, but now it was a jail, and a young man with a cudgel stood guard at the entrance. The boy stepped aside as Croft approached. He looked away when Hutter greeted him.

"It stinks of her," Croft said. "Gird yourself." He removed a cross bar and pulled open the door. The shed was dark on the inside, save for a few lances of sunlight that pierced gaps in the walls. The interior stank of earth and sweat and urine. When Croft called to the girl, his voice deepened with authority. Hutter wondered if the Puritan had commanded when he was a soldier. He had the natural air. "Rosamond Wise," he said. "Stand, girl."

Hutter moved closer for a better look.

Rosamond was a pitiful sight. She stood from the dirt on wobbly, malnourished legs. She was thin as ropes, and just as unsteady. She looked like a starved dog. Life had left her eyes, leaving an abyss in her clouded gaze. She wore a burlap sack for a dress and nothing more. Her feet were bare and blackened. Her hair, dark as ink, hung in knotted clumps, and dry mud braided the locks. Her mouth was a thin line, betraying no feeling. Her nose was wide and swollen and discolored where she'd been struck with a fist. The bruises spread into her eyes.

"Looks like you already worked her over," Wolfric said.

She isn't strong enough to torture, Hutter thought. But then he forced himself to remember her crime. Again, he pictured his children. If dispassionate, he could never do his job well. Anger was a must. He won Croft's respect by taunting the girl. "Shall we have a talk?" he asked.

Rosamond, as if her eyes were painted stones, looked ahead without seeing, emotionless. Though she was a young woman, her hands trembled like those of the elderly. She was ready to die.

"It can't be done in there," Wolfric told Croft. "We need space."

"Of course," Croft said. "We've prepared a spot for you in the woods." Cruelly, he looked at Rosamond. "I'd hate for her screams to disturb the womenfolk."

"Doesn't look like she speaks or screams," Wolfric said.

"She screams," Croft remarked.

Hatchet the roots, wither the tree.

Where Strattonwick met the forest, a thin trail began its labyrinthine route. The trail was wide enough for a single horse and rider, no more. *Walk the trail far enough and you'll end up in the stables of Lord Allingham*, Croft had said, noticeably proud of his lord. The Puritan, bedecked in coat and wide-brimmed hat, led Hutter and Wolfric to a clearing a few hundred yards from the village. There was a scummy pond here, crowned with the refuse of frogs, and there was a pad of trimmed grass surrounded by ancient oak trees. *Our little oasis,* Croft had said. *Idyllic.* Then, as if a busy man, he left the executioners with Rosamond. The Puritan whistled as he went away on the trail, a tuneless hymn, but soon the cavernous forest ate up his melody. It was as if he were making a point.

Rosamond, wrists and ankles bound with twine, backed awkwardly against one of the oaks and slid to the ground. She had yet to make a noise.

"What do you make of Croft?" Hutter asked.

Wolfric shook his head. "One of the truer bastards I've met. Too bad war didn't take more than his hand."

Hutter laughed. "He'd say God spared him."

"Of course, he would. What would the world do without Israel Croft? How would this pile of shit function without his one steady hand and guidance? Reminds me of my time in the lowlands. Did I ever tell you—"

"—He's no soldier." The voice was so alien and unexpected that both Hutter and Wolfric turned, startled.

Rosamond stared forward, still and emotionless, and said no more. It came to Hutter then that the woman never blinked.

"I'll be damned," Wolfric said. "I'll get a fire ready."

Hutter walked to the woman's side and knelt. He had the sick feeling that this woman was capable of lurching and biting him. There was something of the wild animal in her. Still, he remained at her side. "What do you know of Master Croft?" he asked. "What do you make of him? Could it be he chopped off his hand to see what was inside?" This was, he would admit, a highly unusual approach to a quarry one was prepared to put through the pain of torture, but the entire journey had been odd. Strattonwick was odd.

Rosamond did not answer. Being so close to her was like stepping over a corpse. The only life in this woman was vegetable life. *No spirit,* he thought.

Hutter, out of an unwieldy fear more than wisdom, let his next question die without expression. It was irrational and he chastised himself for the thought. He wanted to ask the woman about the mound he'd seen on the forest road, of the sticks moving in the shape of an infant. Why that had come to him, he could not say, but Rosamond inspired the same feelings the mound inspired. She drew him now. The gravity of Rosamond's presence could wither a man's bravado.

Wolfric, eager, had already gone to work building a small fire. Diligently, he raked flint. Soon, smoke curled around his shoulders. When the fire could sustain itself, he retrieved the iron pincers from his satchel. While smiling at Rosamond, he placed the tongs in the flame, letting the utensil roast and turn orange.

"That will happen only if you don't speak," Hutter said, in a tone he generally used on children. In a lower register, he went on. "Ol' Wolf will raise your arms up and pin them. And then he'll take the pincer and put it to your armpit. First the left. When it's hot like that, skin comes off with the slightest pinch. The right arm is next. Is that worth your silence, girl? He'll take a chunk of skin the size of a coin."

Rosamond, despite her effort, began to breathe heavily. The thin line at her mouth trembled. Tears rimmed her eyes.

Wolfric made a show of monitoring the pincers. He gripped the tool and held it aloft, as if testing its readiness. He seemed more ogre than human, and it was an act he enjoyed. Wolfric was capable of great cruelty when his inhibitions were lowered.

Rosamond's next words were almost a chant, spoken like a lyric. "You have the hatchet. Are you its sire?" Rosamond asked. She pointed to the woodsman's tool at Hutter's waist.

"What does that mean?"

"Sire of the Hatchet," Rosamond said, her voice singsong.

"You're speaking nonsense."

Wolfric stood with the glowing pincers.

"Wait," Hutter said. Looking into Rosamond's eyes, he felt the tang of copper at the back of his throat. The tears, when they moved over her bruises, began to change. He saw it happen. He couldn't believe it, but he saw it. The tears turned into dark fleas and leapt from her skin. Instinctively, Hutter jumped back. "What are you?" he asked.

"What's wrong?" Wolfric moved forward with the tongs. "Did she bite you? Lift her arms, damn it."

Breathing heavily, Hutter said, "Wait, I told you. Put it in the fire, Wolf."

"You've lost your mind," Wolfric said. "Or she's hexed you," he muttered.

"What are you?" Hutter asked, inching forward again.

"Hatchet the roots, wither the tree. Sire of the hatchet. Cutter of the cross."

"She's playin' a witch with you," Wolfric said. When the pincers lost their glow, he placed the tool once again in the fire. "You've seen her kind before. A game of the mind," he said. "No doubt that works with Master Croft, but not here, girl."

Hutter could no longer contain his question. "What of the mound?" he asked.

"Codswallop," Wolfric said.

"What of it?" he asked Rosamond.

Rosamond's blank eyes stared forward. She had not blinked and she had not looked at Hutter. It was as if the eyes were blind. "The mother's belly," she said.

"You knew of our journey here?"

Rosamond said nothing.

"The roots?"

"The children."

"Wolf saw the roots following us."

"Indeed, he did. They're worried about me. They're with you more than you know. They were with you in the church."

At that, a great rustling of leaves arose from behind the oaks. The noise formed a circle around the clearing.

Wolfric dropped the pincers. "Jesus God," he said, staring into the shadows. His face went ashen.

At the brink of losing his nerve, Hutter asked, "Did you kill your child?"

"It was not my child," Rosamond said.

"Did you kill him?"

"I did not."

"Did you bury him?"

"Yes. And Croft killed him by digging him up. Croft knows," she said. "Long ago he chopped his wrist to find out."

Unabated, the forest moved around them. Hutter chanced a look behind the oaks. He saw the hard line of a root move like an arm out of sight.

"She confessed to burying it," Wolfric said. "That's enough."

Hutter agreed. He yanked the girl to a standing position. Then, without a word, shoved her towards the trail. Wolfric, unsatisfied with the pace, lifted Rosamond and carried her back to the village.

She said nothing more. Her eyes were dry of tears.

What disturbed you, Puritan?

The site of execution was a large rock that formed a platform by the riverside. The locals, Croft said, called it the Raven Stone, naming it for the carrion that fed on criminals here. There were three sharp pikes stuck in the ground beside the rock, empty of heads, but a reminder to those inclined to malfeasance. "Peasants don't come here," Croft said. "They believe it's haunted." He laughed.

"Who carved all these names?" asked Hutter. He pointed to the myriad etchings that lined the stones: names, mottos, phrases from the Bible, marks like runes.

"Brave children," Croft said. "Children dare each other to come down here at night. It's a rite of passage in Strattonwick."

Hutter stepped onto the unnaturally flat stone. It was not a high perch, but it did give one a more commanding feel over the river. There was peace in the slow current. In the distance, Hutter spied men fishing from the shore, bulking up a feast that would accompany the execution. A breeze moved over the black water and pressed him, carrying the familiar tang of dead fish. From here one could see where the river curled around the forest at the opposite side. On his own side: the plain, the gardens, the hovels of Strattonwick looming above. Croft stood on the ground, peering up with a hint of animosity, accusatory about something. God knew. He blocked the sun with his knobbed forearm. Rosamond had drawn attention to this deformity.

Hutter had left Wolfric behind, allowing the man to get drunk in the quiet of the church. He understood the desire.

"Are you a family man?" Croft asked.

Hutter wished the Puritan would go away. He'd come here to be alone, to think, to be calm after what he'd seen and heard in the forest. He still felt shaken. The image of Rosamond's tears turning to fleas kept him ill. He paced on the stone, like an actor on a stage. "A wife and two sons," he said, noncommittally. "You?" *Puritans*, he thought, *usually have large families.* He'd met Puritans with twenty children. It was sinful to be alone and not reproduce.

Croft took a seat on the edge of the Raven Stone. He fiddled with one of the pikes, twisting it in the loose soil. "In another life," he said. He stopped there, though, and Hutter didn't care to push the matter.

"I can't imagine Strattonwick has much use for this stone," Hutter said.

"About once a generation," Croft admitted. "These pikes are dry-rotted, just for show." He was silent for a moment. The breeze picked up, bending the distant garden. The stench of the river invaded one's senses. "What disturbed you out there?" he asked. "Was it just because you have children? Or did she say things?"

Hutter kept pacing. He refused to look at Croft, to betray his thoughts. It occurred to him that the Puritan wanted to ask, *What did she say about Israel Croft?*

"She admitted to burying the boy, as I told you."

"Did she show you things?"

Guardedly, Hutter asked, "Like what?"

It was clear that Croft was battling his thoughts. He stood and began to walk away, but stopped. "Witchcraft," he said, his voice barely audible in the wind. There was something desperate in his tone, as if, in his life, he'd seen the princes of Hell.

"She's just a frightened girl," Hutter said. "As well she should be." He simply couldn't bring himself to form words about what he'd seen. It was absurd. It couldn't be spoken.

Hutter's reply was not an answer, but Croft didn't push. "At dusk," he said, "we'll begin the feast. I want the deed done with now, not tomorrow. Are you willing?"

Hutter nodded, relieved. He dreaded another night of waiting. *They were with you in the church*, Rosamond had taunted. "We'll be ready," Hutter said.

Croft began a trek towards the gardens where young men toiled, leaving Hutter alone on the Raven Stone. The old man moved so oddly, so disjointed.

She said you weren't a soldier, Hutter thought, but then reminded himself that Croft never claimed to be. *She was in my mind. Not yours.* Hutter turned to the river. *What disturbed you, Puritan?* he thought.

There was once a woodsman. Hutter opened the door of the church and stepped into the shade. A haze of heat hung in the air. The air was stagnant and smelled of sweat. "Wolf?" he called, scanning the pews. "The Puritan wants it done today." *And thank God for it*, he thought. He moved up the aisle to the altar, where there stood a simple wooden cross, unpainted and austere with splinters. The cross was the only ornamentation in the entire building. From the front of the room, he looked about for Wolfric, but there was no sign of the man. The church was silent, save for Hutter's breathing. He walked again towards the sunlight of the open door, checking on the floor for an unconscious, drunken Wolfric. There was no sign he'd been here at all. Their satchels remained undisturbed in the Harlot Pews.

Outside, Hutter saw a youth watching him. He waved the boy over, but the child, taught to be ashamed of speaking to such a man, ducked his head and turned away. Perturbed, Hutter followed. "Boy," he said. "Just a question for you."

The child, no more than ten, with a moon face and unkempt red hair, halted. He kept his back turned.

Hutter spoke to him without looking in his face. "Have you seen the man I travel with? The large man with a blond beard."

The boy nodded.

A woman, stout and crusted with filth, hurried towards the boy. Without looking at Hutter, she took the child's hand. "Don't speak to him," she said. "You'll soil all of us."

"Where'd you see him?" Hutter asked, trying to keep his temper down in the face of such an insult.

"He went to the forest," the child called. The woman smacked the boy's face, hard.

Hutter stood alone, a waft of smoke obscuring his vision. *The forest?* he thought. *Not even Wolf would be such a fool as that.* Hutter started towards the trail at the rear of Strattonwick, the trail that led to Lord Allingham, the trail that led to the spot where Rosamond had called him Sire of the Hatchet. In haste, he cut through a pit of mud between two hovels. The muck nearly ripped off his boots.

The child had not been lying. Indeed, there sat Wolfric, on the incline where the trail began, his back to the shed that housed Rosamond, his arms draped over his knees. The guard with the cudgel was nowhere in sight. Hutter approached. Wolfric didn't seem drunk; his gaze was too aware, too inward.

"What are you doing?" Hutter asked.

"Waiting on you," he said. Gone was the vicious tone, the vitriol. Wolfric spoke flatly, as a man traumatized. "I have something to show you."

"The Puritan wants it done today," Hutter said. "I thought that would please you. Is the girl in there?"

Wolfric shrugged. "You're not listening to me. I want to show you something."

"What is it?" He noticed now that dry mud caked Wolfric's hands.

Wolfric stood. There was no evidence he had had anything to drink. He was too steady. "Follow me," he said. "Those things aren't here. At least they're hiding themselves better now. And it isn't far."

"Who's guarding the girl?"

"After what you saw, that isn't a sensible question. She chooses to stay."

Hutter could not argue with that.

Wolfric led Hutter past the oasis where they had interrogated Rosamond. For Hutter, there was still a residue in the air here. The feeling moved beneath his skin. He turned his gaze from the oily surface of the pond. The trail forked. To one side, the path led onward, deeper into the forest. To the other side, the path opened into a fenced clearing, a cemetery with simple wooden crosses. Wolfric looked at his hands. "It was the only fresh grave," he said.

"What have you done?" Such an abomination shook Hutter to the core. His anger swelled.

"I had to see," Wolfric said. He would not be intimidated. The larger of the two, he reached out and gripped Hutter's arm. "You have to see."

Hutter struggled to free his arm but couldn't break Wolfric's iron grasp. He stopped short of striking his assistant, but his anger remained high. Wolfric pulled him through the graves and crosses, stamping with disrespect over the bodies in the earth. The grave was at the back corner beneath the fence, a mark of the unbaptized. Wolfric had not replaced the dirt in the infant's grave. Earth and stone remained piled at the side.

A stained shroud covered what lay at the bottom of the hole.

"It's very real," Wolfric said. He released Hutter's arm. "She did not lie to you."

"I didn't ask for proof," Hutter said.

"Here. Look." Wolfric knelt and pulled back the hardened shroud. A faint trace of moss had begun to grow over the cloth. "There's no smell," Wolfric said. "No rot. Just the smell of the dirt."

Of the mound, Hutter thought. *Almost pleasant.*

Although a black, peeling layer of skin covered the skull and erupted in swaths over the body, there were other areas of the child exposed. Rather than bones, tree roots formed a skeleton beneath the flesh. It occurred to Hutter that the infant had been growing flesh, and that the process was incomplete. The child had no nose and no more than a lanced boil for a mouth.

Wolfric touched one of the legs. "Light as kindling," he marveled. "Just sticks. Like a doll."

There was another presence in their midst. Hutter started. His heart was hard against his chest. He turned, expecting the Puritan to be standing among the crosses. It was not Israel Croft whom he saw, but Rosamond Wise. She gripped a hatchet, not unlike the one Hutter wore, and there was blood up her arm. The blood, he could see, was her own. There was a wound on her forearm as wide and wet as an open mouth. Mites scuttled from the gash.

"You see now?" she asked.

Hutter wanted to turn away, but he was mesmerized by the woman's approach. He couldn't look away. Wolfric, still on his knees, his mind battered, began to weep.

Rosamond handed the hatchet to the executioner. She did so with calmness. She lay her wounded arm across the fence. "Take one of the fingers," she said. "Sire of the hatchet," she purred. "Cutter of the cross."

"Why do you call me that?"

"There once was a woodsman," she started, as if she were telling a story to a child, but left the thought unfinished.

Hutter, delirious, gripped the hatchet. As instructed, he brought down the blade against one of her fingers. When the blow was done, the finger severed, Rosamond recoiled in pain. Tears rimmed her eyes, and each turned to a flea and bounded forth into the woods. She did not cry out, although she felt agony as anyone would feel it.

Wolfric picked the finger from the pile of grave dirt. He wiped the blood on his shirt. "No bone," he said. He wiped the tears from his face. "Just a piece of the root."

Madness, Hutter thought, but he looked. Indeed, the still warm flesh encased a dark, splintering root. His stomach grew sick, his head light.

"Leave us," Rosamond said. Her hand, although she gripped it tightly, bled profusely. Her face was ghastly white, her thin lips colorless.

Hutter helped Wolfric from the ground. The assistant, he noticed, placed the severed finger in his pocket. Rosamond did not object. What could be hidden now? As the two men, absorbed and silent, moved through the graves, Rosamond went to her knees. She began to sweep dirt into the child's grave with her undamaged hand. And now she was weeping, too.

In the boughs of a sprawling tree, Hutter saw the skeletal movements of other infants, moving with the deftness of felines. With the knots of their eyes, he presumed, they watched, but they did not interfere.

Who, here, knows their mother?

A crowd gathered by the river in Strattonwick, but there was no feast. Tables had not been brought forth. There were no fire pits to prepare the fish or roast the vegetables. The sun was at its pinnacle and the day was hot. No one spoke or bustled for space. Tension laced the air. The men and women and children, poor, dirt-caked peasants, God-fearing, demon-haunted, simply stood and looked on at the Raven Stone in wonder, as they would've done if Jesus Christ lowered from the clouds. There were nearly forty villagers. The river behind the stone moved slowly, unchanged. The sun shone over the oily water. The boat that would have been used for drowning Rosamond Wise lay against the shore, punched into the mud. There was a large and empty burlap sack in the vessel. None of these things drew the attention of the villagers. It was the grisly vision upon the Raven Stone that arrested their minds. The sight would either turn the villagers pious or make them debauched. Time would tell.

The blood seemed like nothing to them. Other, more personal, details brought them horror.

Hutter and Wolfric, emerging from the forest, traipsing through lines of hovels, passing through the gardens, caused no disturbance in this gathering by the river's edge. Their presence was unheeded. Nor did the executioner and his assistant speak to one another once the sight was clear. What was there to say? What could ever be said? There would only be the images, sights like this.

The villagers, and now Hutter and Wolfric, gazed in awe upon the work of Rosamond's hatchet.

Master Croft, his Puritan shield of brown cloth removed, his flesh splayed, razored open, lay across the stone in a pool of blood. How she had overpowered him, or even caught the old man by surprise, was unclear. Maybe the roots in the forest did more than watch. The Puritan's head had been severed, cut without precision from his shoulders. Where the skin had been removed from his body, where bones should have protruded, there was only a system of roots. The sinew at his neck looked like vines, the meat like wet moss.

He, too, Hutter thought, awed. *Who, here, knows their mother? Who else has severed a piece of their body to learn?*

Wolfric, dazed, retrieved Rosamond's finger from his pocket. He examined the digit closely, like a Catholic with his relic, preferring it to the sight of Croft.

Hutter wondered if his companion would ever regain his mind. "There's nothing for us here," Hutter whispered. He took Wolfric by the arm and tried to lead him, but the man was too stubborn, too strong. He separated from Hutter's grasp and melted into the crowd of villagers.

Hutter looked to the forest road, so near, and felt dread. The road passed the mound, the mother's belly. He would have to look upon the knoll once more, and he'd have to do so with nothing more than a hatchet.

⚒

SAM HICKS

BACK ALONG THE OLD TRACK

IT'S funny, but I can't remember how the game ended, or if it ended at all, but I do remember that I had just set my last but one domino on the old wooden counter, and that Tom Ranscomb was chuckling softly as he looked at the piece he held shielded in his hand. I don't remember if he was amused by victory or defeat, because then someone said, "There they all go," and in such comically doom-laden tones that I turned from our game to see what was meant. Outside the deep bay windows of the Old King's Inn a hearse was rolling past. It was moving at little above walking pace, slow enough to accommodate the black clad mourners following on foot. A dense tumble of greenery, mainly ivy I think, was heaped over the coffin, piled so high that a great deal had spilled into the cavity around, snaking up the windows as if it were growing still. Ten people followed the car, amongst them two small children, heads bowed and hands clasped tightly, prayer-like, in front.

There was a stir of interest in the public bar and some whispered comments that I couldn't quite catch.

"Whose funeral?" I asked Tom.

"That'll be old John Sleator's." He leaned on the counter with his arms straight and the fingers of his big hands spread, watching the procession with narrowed eyes. "About time too, some would say."

Tom was the landlord of the pub and of the holiday cottage I was renting—and a man whose words you listened to. He was intelligent, well read, and possessed an air of calm sagacity, born, I liked to think, of a lifetime's study of the human dramas played out in his domain. So although I was surprised to hear him make such an unkind comment I was prepared to believe it wasn't lightly said. He continued: "They'll be in here later for the wake, in the back room. Sleators have always held their wakes at the Old King's."

"How long's always?" I asked.

"This pub's been here since 1453 and so have the Sleator family, though *they* were here even before then. That's how long always is, young man. Now—do you need another drink, because I'd better get those sandwiches laid out? Best pack the dominos away. Don't want them catching us engaged in madcap frolic."

I ordered another beer. I had been meaning to leave after our game, but now I wanted to stay and take a look at the Sleators. After ten minutes or so Tom reappeared and said to me: "Now, when they come in, make sure you don't catch any of their eyes."

"Right. Are they really that bad?"

"Not always, but I'd advise caution where Sleators are concerned. Just in case. Everyone in here knows about them, but you, being a visitor, don't."

One of the old men playing cards at a corner table, and clearly not hard of hearing, spoke up. "You'll do well to listen to Tom, young'un. I still got some lively scars from the day I looked at a Sleator wrong. Here—you know you can see their farm across the field at the back of your cottage?'

"That place? That's theirs?"

"Oh, yes," Tom said. "Lucky for you there's a field in between. You're out of harm's way, don't worry."

"Is it their field?"

"Oh, yes. But you've seen it. They don't pay it much mind. Mainly they raise goats and brew cider from their orchard. We sell it in here, the cider. People come from miles around to drink Sleator Special."

"Knock your socks of that will," said a grizzled man sitting on his own near the door.

"And you'd know all about that, Arthur," said Tom.

The public bar of the Old King's Inn was small, making a private conversation difficult when, as on that day, so few people were there. I wanted to question Tom further about this notorious family, but was held back by the thought of being overheard. Had it been the weekend (which was when I'd first arrived) it would have been a different matter. Then the pub would be packed with people from surrounding towns come to enjoy its unchanging rustic charms, the low beamed ceilings, the thick cave-like walls, open stone fireplaces and the barrels of beer stacked up behind the bar. Then, even the back room would be lively with shouts and laughter, and the Sleators and their funereal gloom would be far from anyone's mind.

As Tom said, I was a visitor, yet even an outsider could sense the tension growing in the room. No one left and little was said. Tom took to wiping things down behind the counter and quite unnecessarily, I suspected, to counting the takings in the till, filling small bags with the coppers and silvers and replacing them in the drawer with an impatient sigh. Then a blast of March air put an end to the vigil, as the door swung open so abruptly that it bounced off the frame with a splintering crack. Tom winced.

"Everything's ready," he said. "Just go through."

I didn't turn my head after the warning I'd received, but I watched the party as they trooped past the end of the counter, through the low door and into the crooked passage that lead to the back room. There was no missing the family resemblance in the three generations, although it was split between two types. The three younger men, one of the older men, and a woman I placed in her late sixties, represented one branch of the clan. They had heavy, prominent, simian jaws which didn't quite fit with the high narrow foreheads and small sunken eyes above. The other older man and the two younger women had flat, mask-like faces with squashed noses and thick-lidded, watery eyes. The children, perhaps aged five or six, had these same liquid eyes and already a marked thickening around their chins. An unpleasant thought occurred to me and when they were all safely out of hearing I said to Tom in an undertone: "Close-knit lot, aren't they?"

Tom raised an eyebrow and leaned across the counter. "So you noticed that, eh? Sleators marry Burchards and Burchards marry Sleators and if your cousin is your third or your second or your first or even your half-sister, well who's counting? The little ones haven't become one or the other yet, but they always do. They don't combine, you see. One side always gets the upper hand and then the face comes out. The Sleators have that Cro-Magnon look and the Burchards look like fish. Oh yes, you see it all out here. And you thought all the excitement was to be had in the city."

For all Tom's counsel, a few minutes later I did just the thing he had warned me not to. Before leaving I needed to pay a visit to the gents', which were situated perilously close to the back room, just off the connecting passageway. When I emerged from that tomb-like chamber, I simply couldn't resist a glance through the open door. Emotions were clearly running high. One of the older men, he with the Sleator looks, had pulled one of the younger male Sleators towards him by the lapels of his funeral jacket and was shouting in his befuddled face. "You should know what to do by now you mangy idiot! You're less use than a turd! I'll have to take care of it myself then, won't I?" The rest of the party looked on, not shocked by the man's behavior but rather approving of it, it seemed to me. The senior Sleator tossed the younger one aside, sending him crashing into the table where Tom had set up plates of sandwiches and bottles of cider and beer. Then, swearing loudly, he pushed his way out of the room, only to meet the eye of the puny stranger cowering just beyond the threshold. If it weren't for his obvious distraction, I am certain he would have punched me in the face there and then, but as it was, he shoved past me, uttering something like a growl. I was shaking when I returned to the bar.

"You just met Jacob Sleator, didn't you?" said Tom, when he saw me. "Cheer up. You're still alive."

I took the scenic route back to the cottage, over a field and through Larke Woods, the box of dry food that Tom had given me for Sanderson rattling in my bag as I went. Sanderson was a big bruiser of a ginger cat who lived in the wood shed behind the house. Tom Ranscomb fed and cared for Sanderson, a stray, but had utterly failed to persuade him to move into his flat on the first floor of the Old King's Inn. Sanderson preferred his independence and his bed in an orange crate full of rags and wadding to life as a bachelor's companion. Tom said he hoped Sanderson might change his mind when he got to be an elderly cat, that he might see the wisdom of pooling resources, but that for now he was resistant to logic. As soon as I was back, I filled Sanderson's enamel bowl with the food and called for him. But then I spotted him over near the dustbin by the kitchen door. He was hunkered down, patting lazily at some small creature in the grass, so completely possessed by that feline mix of playfulness and cruelty that he was oblivious to my presence. I shouted at him and advanced, hoping to rescue the bird or mouse from a slow death by torture. Sanderson looked up, amazed to see me there, and scooted away through the hedge into what I now knew to be the Sleator's field. I squatted down to assess the condition of his prey, then leapt straight back up with a yelp. Armed with a stout twig, I approached again. It wasn't easy to say what it was. It was as white as squid, with the same slimy gloss, but as thick and muscular as a steak. The shape I can only compare to a hugely magnified wheat berry, pointed at the ends and fatter in the center, slightly convex at its widest point. It lay oozing a thin grey liquid that shimmered as it leaked into the grass. Perhaps Sanderson had got his claws on the afterbirth of some farm animal, I thought. I prodded it with the twig then lifted it towards the dustbin. As I dropped it in, it twitched. Retching a bit, I banged down the lid and wiped my hands on my trousers even though I had not actually touched the thing.

I had by then cancelled my plans to drive into the nearest town for dinner that night. It struck me as far too much effort, and I was instead looking forward to a cozy night basking in the warmth of the cast iron wood burner, some soup and bread, maybe a glass or two of wine and bed before ten. That, after all, was the idea of staying there—I'd intended walks on the High Weald, early nights, wholesome food, peace and quiet. I could just as easily have had a couple of weeks in Italy or Greece or France instead of the safe option of rural Kent, but I felt tired just thinking about airports and taxis and museum crowds and hire cars and other languages and trudging along endless dusty, incomprehensible streets. I needed, at that particular time, familiarity, snugness, ease. I'd been working too hard for too long and after one incident too many of losing my temper with someone I shouldn't have, I finally took my head of department's advice to have some time away. A friend of mine recommended the cottage in the hamlet of Mardham. She'd stayed there one Christmas. "It was bliss," she said. "One pub, one church, one shop. Houses that really look like gingerbread. And everyone was so nice."

As dusk fell, it started to rain. I hoped Sanderson had recovered from the shock I'd given him and returned to the shelter of his little nest in the shed. I looked out the kitchen window as I stirred the soup on the hob, checking for signs of him. At the end of the strip of lawn the high blackthorn hedge, still winter bare, for it had been a cold late spring, revealed scraps of the field beyond. Where the ground rose in the distance I could see the ramshackle metal barn, randomly patched with bits of wood. Behind it was the buckled roof of the house, a narrow ribbon of smoke rising from one of its four chimneys. Tom Ranscomb was right about the field—the Sleators didn't appear to pay it much mind. Earlier in the week I'd balanced on an upturned bucket to look over the hedge, curious to see if a crop was growing there, but was left none the wiser. Nothing there but a collection of diseased grey seed heads rising from collapsed rosettes of leaves, patches of thistle and rough weed, claggy earth and stones.

The fading light and the rain lent a greyness to everything that evening—a dreary sodden aspect that made me glad to be indoors. The radio burbled from the mantelpiece and the simmering soup, bought from a city deli, smelt good. Then I saw something walking past the hedge in the Sleator's field. The parts that were visible through the twisted thorn darkened, then lightened, then darkened again. I was sure it was a person. The person had to be a Sleator. With the unruffled movements of someone unaware they are being watched, I carried the soup pan to the table and then returned to the window, pulling the chintz curtains shut in a casual, everyday way. If they couldn't see me, I couldn't see them.

But I couldn't let it go. For the rest of the evening I was as jittery as a rabbit who knows a fox has caught its scent. I forensically analyzed any unexpected sound, turned the radio down at every creak and crack of old timber and brick and checked that the doors were locked again and again, in case I'd been mistaken the last time. I pictured a Sleator lurking outside, waiting for me to emerge so he could inflict lively scars upon me as had happened to the man in the pub. I had, after all, caught Jacob Sleator's eye. Perhaps he would come for revenge and I could only guess at what he might think suitable. In the end the wine and the warmth of the sitting room stupefied me sufficiently for sleep, and I tottered up the narrow stairs to the bedroom I had made my own. I went to draw the curtains and paused when I noticed that the rain had stopped and a perfect full moon was shining, dazzling, over the Sleators' field. And there, at the brow of the hill, I saw a hunched figure with a coil of thick rope slung around his upper body, laboring, head down, towards the barn. He passed into the shadow of some trees and was gone.

━━━━━━━━━━━━━━━

I rose late the next morning and had a proper fried breakfast, washed down with several cups of strong coffee, and seeing as it was a cheerful blue-skied day, set off for a walk along the river and past the old mill ponds that were dotted around the outskirts of the village. I checked the shed before I left,

but there was no sign of Sanderson and his food looked un-
touched; but I was pretty sure there was no cause for alarm
with a cat like that. I laughed at the state I'd got myself in the
night before. For God's sake, I told myself, you live in a city
where you take your life in your hands every time you walk
home at night, and here you get jumpy at a shadow behind a
hedge. It was, after all, only extraordinary circumstances that
had led me to know of the Sleators' existence, and in all likeli-
hood I wouldn't see them again before I went home.

It was possible, I'd been told, to walk in a circle from my
cottage, through meadows and small orchards and scraps of
copse, whilst never leaving the banks of some water course or
another. The area had once been home to several watermills
and a leather dying industry, remembered in names like
Tanner's Lane and Mill Road and the first stream I was to
follow, the Mill Leat. I found this stretch of water, sheeny,
leaf-clogged, barely moving, at the edge of a meadow that was
halfway turned to liquid mud. A comparatively dry footbridge
at the far corner took me over a white swirling weir, and then I
was on the bank of the little river Chase, whose maundering,
sedimented course I followed for the next mile or so. The
path then cut away from the bank through sharp hawthorn
thickets, past scatterings of leafless apple trees, and on to skirt
round pastures whispering with the bubbling, licking sounds
of watery earth. I passed a series of ponds covered in floating
islands of broken reeds, a collapsed and abandoned tractor
trailer, a pile of man-sized concrete pipes, moss-grown and
forgotten in a field, and then I was again by the river, crossing
a rusty metal bridge back in the direction of the village. My
hope had been that a walk would lift my spirits but in fact
it seemed to have left me feeling a bit demoralized, perhaps
due to the effects of the sludge underfoot and the sluggish,
despondent look of the landscape in those few square miles.
Even the willow branches overhanging the river held snags
of decaying vegetation, circling in the breeze like the corpses
of tattered birds. Knowing that the final section of any walk
always seems the longest, I increased my pace, which wasn't

easy with boots plastered with wads of grass and mud. Then I came to a sudden stop. A deep masculine shout rang out, as clear as a cannon, from somewhere back the way I came. But it was more of a bellow than a shout; aggressive, full of guttural threat, the kind deployed to scare a savage animal away. Nightmare images of violent pursuit sprang panting into my mind—bloody wounds and matted fur, yellow teeth bared in gruesome slavering mouths. I pictured the crazed dread of the animal as it tore through the spiked thickets, headlong, dangerous like the man giving chase, prey and predator deadly to anything which crossed their paths. Having turned myself lightheaded with fear, I broke into something near a jog, and didn't dare slow for the last half mile, not until the path turned back to the lane where my cottage was. My breath was still ragged when I walked into the back garden and saw, framed in the open door of the shed, the goblin form of a Sleator child.

I recognized it as the larger of the two I had seen in the Old King's Inn. My guess was that it was a boy from the cut of the stiff hair, but the features of the child were ambiguous to say the least. He gazed at me listlessly and stretched out a stubby arm.

"I was looking," he said.

For a moment I was at a total loss. What did you do in situations like that?

"Is your…daddy here?" I ventured. "Or mummy? Someone?"

I went to the back door and found it locked as I had left it.

The child began to sniffle. "I was looking," he whimpered.

"Well, that's alright," I said. "Looking's alright. Now how did you get here? Do mummy and daddy know you're here?"

He shook his head and pawed his cheeks with his shrimpy fingers.

What the hell was I meant to do? Of all the kids that could end up in my woodshed, why this one? One thing I was sure of was that I was not going to be the one to return it to the Sleator farm. Then I thought of Tom. I only had to get the child to Tom. He'd know what to do.

"Now, I bet your mummy and daddy are looking for you. We'll go and see Tom at the Old King's—you know, where you were yesterday? And then he'll get your mummy. How about that?"

The child nodded, staring at me with a sort of awe. I suppose he was trying to work out what I was—Sleator or Burchard, or something entirely wonderful and new. I got him to follow me to my car, strapped him into the front seat (feeling exactly like an abductor) and drove the half mile to the pub.

There was only one punter in the public bar, much to my relief—an ancient, flat-capped fellow, lingering over the dregs of his beer. Tom Ranscomb was behind the counter, drying a glass, holding it up to the light for smears, humming a merry tune to himself. When he saw me, he put the glass down with care.

"Well, now. What's all this?" he said.

I went up to the bar and slid onto one of the high stools.

"Tom, I've just found a Sleator child in my woodshed. He's outside in my car. I didn't know what to do."

Tom scratched his head and blew through his teeth. "Now let's see. Take him back?"

"I know, I know, but what with them being a bit hostile—"

"You wondered if I might do it instead?"

"Well, I thought it might be better. But you could phone them couldn't you? Then they could come and get him."

"Hmm. Thing is, they don't have a phone. Barely got electricity. And the thing is, they'll know you found him soon enough and they'll wonder why you didn't take him back yourself. And we don't want Sleators set all a-wonder. So what I suggest is I come with you and we'll return the errant child together. How about that? Just give me a minute to lock up."

I'd rather hoped not to involve myself at all but I deferred to Tom's judgment.

I wasn't in the least surprised that there was a handmade "Keep Out" sign at the start of the potholed drive that led to the Sleator place. The drive branched off a narrow lane that ran past the tiny medieval church and graveyard. I'd already walked the lane and discovered that soon after the church it became unsurfaced track through apple orchards, narrowing to a dirt path that led up Mardham Hill. The child sat quietly in the back seat as I drove, sniffing every now and then. I thought he was probably enjoying his little adventure.

"You better wait here," Tom said when we pulled up in the yard in front of the house. "I'll see if anyone's about."

I nodded assent as I looked at the smashed windows on the ground floor of the dirt-colored building, the door swinging on one hinge, the bits of clothing and pots and pans and glass strewn around the muddy concrete yard.

"Christ!" I said. "What the hell's been going on here?"

"Sleators been going on here," Tom replied.

I watched him go up to the house and call out. When no answer came, he walked round the side, probably to check the barn. I didn't like him being out of sight—what if they turned up now, and me with their child in the back of the car? The yard was situated behind the miserable field that backed onto my cottage, and through a gap in the trees—stricken, wind-sheared things—I could see the upper floor and the humped clay tiles of the roof. I sat forward in my seat. Through the gaps of the hedge I could see something white, moving slowly, in a way that even from there was suggestive of a living thing. A big hand thumped onto my nearside window and the door behind me clicked. It was Tom. Across the yard, hovering at the side of the house, was the Sleator matriarch, her arms crossed over her old khaki sweater, her face set in an inexplicable expression of defiance.

"Come on littl'un," Tom said, helping the child from the back seat. "Grandma's waiting for you."

The boy hopped out and scampered over to the woman, who made no move to hug him or even ruffle his hair. Instead, she kept her eyes on Tom and me as I started the engine and reversed the car out of the yard.

"Well?" I asked him, as we jolted back up the track. "Why was the house all smashed up? And had they even noticed the kid was gone?"

Tom shook his head wearily. "What can I tell you? I asked her if there'd been any trouble and do you know what she says? Ha! She tells me a goat got out the top field and went a bit mad. That's where the rest of them are, she says, putting the mad goat back in the field. Little Adam must've wandered off in all the fuss, she says."

"A goat? A goat that rips doors off and needs a whole gang of Sleators to restrain it?"

He looked at me and sighed. "What can I say? I'd like to say it'd be nice for them to do something normal for a change, but I suppose the shock'd kill me if they did. Now, how about a whiskey in the pub before you head back? On the house?"

I said I would pass on the offer, but agreed to go to the Old King's Inn that evening. Tom promised me free beer "to make up for all this fuss."

Back at the cottage, I inspected the garden for evidence of an animal having been there, particularly a white one, but there was nothing I could see, not even Sanderson. I reminded myself to let Tom know that the cat had made himself scarce. Perhaps someone in the village had seen him. Perhaps he'd moved in somewhere else. But maybe he was sick— perhaps that stuff he'd got hold of didn't agree with him. I cautiously lifted the dustbin lid to have another look at it, but either it had sunk down into the rest of the rubbish or it had dried up into the shrivelled black curl of stuff that lay on top of yesterday's papers.

I ended up passing a pleasant evening in the Old King's. I got roped into game after game of euchre (which luckily I'd played a few times before) with three of the old boys and what with the generous supply of beer from Tom, the gruff, sarcastic banter, and the soothing crackle of the log fire, I wandered back to the cottage with the satisfied feeling of a few hours well spent. There had been, however, one moment of awkwardness, although I swept it aside at the time—

when I returned from the bar after a pause in play, my three companions cut short a hushed conversation. The last few words sounded like "one more day" but I wouldn't have dreamed of asking what they meant.

I went up to bed relaxed and content and fell asleep straight away, only to come awake some hours later—horribly, coldly, certain that someone was in the house. I lay rigid, listening to a sound which may have been just outside my bedroom door—a prolonged, yawning creak like a slice of floorboard being prised from the frame below. As if sensing I was now fully conscious, the noise stopped. I clenched the blankets, staring into the dark, until my awareness of every sound, and then of the mournful, hollow circling of the wind outside, reached such an unendurable pitch that I leapt from the bed, smacking the light switch on and slamming the bedroom door to and fro with a cry of "I can hear you! I can hear you!" Silence answered me. But I detected a change, a lifting of pressure, a new texture, as if what had been there had now gone. I turned the light back off and went to the window, opening the curtains a crack. Out there, in the almost phosphorescent light of the moon, I saw two figures crossing Sleator's field and one of them, I am sure, turned briefly, as if he knew I were there.

━━━━━━━━━━

As I made a late breakfast the next morning, I started to toy with the idea of cutting my holiday short. But then I became annoyed with myself for letting my over-anxious nature get the better of me, for giving way to the imagined rather than the actual, as was my habitual wont. So I came to a compromise with myself. I'd give it one more day and if I still couldn't find it in me to relax, I'd admit defeat. I knew I couldn't expect a refund for the remaining days, nor would I ask, but if I was going to spend half the night jumping out of my skin, I would be better off at home. I decided to spend the day further afield and, after another futile search for Sanderson (who Tom assured me often did disappearing acts), I set off for the nearest quaint Kentish town. I visited churches and antique shops. I had tea and cake served to me by girls in black dresses and white aprons. I dawdled in a local history museum. I bought a book on smuggling in the 17th century, and I had dinner in a lovely restaurant with views of a fine church tower. Then I drove back through the unlit country roads in a lighthearted mood, looking forward to a tot or two of the 15-year-old rum I'd bought from a little shop in a honey-colored market square.

I parked the car outside the cottage but I didn't get out. Instead I sat listening to the impatient tick of the cooling engine, reluctant to move at all. "Stupid!" I shouted and I gathered up my bags decisively and went around to the back of the house. But I couldn't shake the unease. I went to the woodshed and fetched the axe that was kept next to the pile of logs. Insurance, I told myself. Who wouldn't sleep easier with an axe under the bed?

The back door was unlocked. No need to panic, I thought, no need. Didn't you forget to lock it once last week? Yes, yes you did. Thought you'd done it but you hadn't. Putting down my bags, but not the axe, I felt for the light switch inside the door. The bulb flickered and extinguished with a snap and in that brief moment I saw illuminated as if by lightning, the gurning, malevolent features of Jacob Sleator and a Sleator son, bent over someone huge and ghastly white into whom they were aiming brutal, driving blows. In the dark, the room seemed to drag itself towards me. Everything dropped from height and crashed into the ground, churned and broken, then rose flying upwards in a furious squall. A mass of flesh smashed into me, crushing me into the wall, surrounding me with choking stench, the smell of dung and airless earth and diseased breath. Then it spun away, barreling through the open door with the others, out into the night.

I stumbled in panic to the kitchen, shoved a chair up against the door and felt my way to the window. Even though what I then witnessed is burnt into my mind, even though I see it again and again in paralyzing, death-like dreams, despite all this I still question how we can ever know if our memories are truly real. I mean the quivering heave of the wet, white flesh that the Sleators were battling to restrain. The fluttering of the root-like fingers, the flailing, clotted, swollen arms and bowed, half-melted legs. The distorted head which juddered through restless attempts at features—a nose that spasmed into the form of an eye, an ear that emptied into a mouth. Jacob Sleator, horribly cut and bruised about the face, had managed to tie some rope around the thing's upper half, and the Sleator son, unflinching, was throwing his own rope over its head. With a united grunting effort they pulled their ends of rope tight, penning the creature between them, and dragged its spasming body to a newly hacked gash in the hedge, through into the rotten furrows of their moonlit field.

Tom was still clearing up in the bar after closing when I banged on the side door, shouting fit to wake the whole village, which I no doubt did. He ushered me to a table near the fire, brought me a double brandy and told me to slow down, to try to get my words right, to take a deep breath. After listening to my muddled, near-delirious account of what happened at the cottage, he rose from the table to fetch the rest of the brandy and a glass for himself. His eyes were troubled when he sat back down, but his manner was as steady as ever.

"Now, then. First things first," he said, filling our glasses. "Did you contact the police at all before you came over here? Did you call them?"

It was a sensible and practical question. I should've done that, and felt embarrassed to admit I hadn't. "No…I suppose my first thought was to get somewhere I'd be safe. But we can call them now. We should do that right away!' I stood up and felt for my phone, but as I pulled it from my pocket Tom said:

"And what will you tell them? You see, that's why I asked. What would you say to them or anyone? That the Sleators were fighting with a monster in your cottage? Is that what you'd tell them?'

I couldn't grasp what he was saying and went on the defensive, waving my arms about to press my point home.

"But that's what it was like! You didn't see it! You can't imagine what it was like! I don't know what it was…something sick, some sick, deformed thing."

"A goat."

I gaped at Tom, feeling totally exasperated. Was he making fun of me? Did he think I'd exaggerated what I'd seen? Was his look of concern the sort he wore professionally to soothe hysterics and madmen and drunks?

"It wasn't a goat. It really, *really* wasn't a goat." I said.

He drew his chair closer to the fireplace, and studied what was left of the logs in the basket grate. Then he turned and spoke.

"Let me tell you something," he said. "Around here we have a saying: "Three days to lay a Sleator to rest." And do you know why? The Sleators, well…they don't…die right. Never have. They die twice, you see. What's buried in the graveyard behind the church isn't what gets burnt to ash and cast upon the ground in their orchard back along the old track. I can't change that and nor can they and it's not for me or anyone else to say as we should. We leave them be and things go on quite well. In a place like this you make allowances; you have to or life becomes unbearable and that's how it is. It's just a shame you happened along when one of them decided to pass and got you caught up in something you shouldn't have been. It's a pity, that is. It isn't always like that, but John Sleator was one of the worst of them and was bound to go hard."

I studied his face, hoping his solemn expression would suddenly break into laughter, willing him to slap his big hand on the table and shout, "Oh, I had you going there!" But that didn't happen. He looked entirely, frighteningly, serious as he sat waiting for me to speak.

"Tom—do you mean it? But how can they die twice? What was that thing? How can they die twice? What was it I saw?'

"I can't explain that in any way you'd like to hear or in any way that would do you any good. So I say it was a goat. A goat got loose. That's what *they'd* say. And that's what I'd say to anyone that asked. You being a worried sort of bloke, got confused in the dark. When people from the city come down here, that can happen. They're just not used to the dark."

And he poured us both another brandy and we sat, not speaking, watching the end of the fire, ash falling like paper onto the worn stone of the hearth, the last dying forks of blue-yellow flame.

LINDSAY KING-MILLER

THE
FRUIT

EVERY year the posters go up earlier and earlier—a certain sign that summer is over. No one ever sees who hangs them, but one day they appear on every bulletin board and telephone pole in town. "Seasonal Work, Overtime Available. Inquire at Genesis Farms." There is no address or telephone number or email.

It is not a job offer. It is a summons.

No one picks up a check at the end of the harvest. We accept payment in the form of being allowed to return home, to huddle indoors through the winter and pretend only the wind is howling outside.

Living this close to the trees, we learn to fear the touch of wood. Our houses are built of brick or stone. We cover our floorboards with carpet or rugs or whatever threadbare blankets we can find. Even as children we do not climb trees.

Every year the trees are taller, and every year we swear there are more of them, though that can't be: we are promised this much, that no new seeds will be planted, as long as we do our duty. We have never seen a sapling reach from the earth. If we did, we would rip it out with our bare hands, no matter what it did when it touched our skin. And yet, each time we return to the orchard, we find it closer to our doors than we remember.

━━━━━━━━━━━

It is still August when Evelyn hears the branches creaking and knows the fruit is growing heavy, though the leaves have not yet turned. When the posters appear, she is ready. Her harvesting knife is sharp, sharp.

Ada brings the ladder from the garage and inspects it carefully. She tightens each screw until her hand burns, then loosens them all and tightens them again. She brings out the steel cleats, her own addition, to dig into the soil so the ladder will never slip. Sometimes the trees like to bend and dodge— sometimes the branch you were leaning on a minute ago is suddenly somewhere else. Any fall in the orchard is a bad fall. Any broken skin is an opening. So Ada is determined that Evelyn will never fall.

Everyone works in pairs: one to hold the ladder and one to climb. Most partners trade off from tree to tree, or day to day. Evelyn insists that Ada stay on the ground. She knows people notice and talk about it, that some women even use it to needle their own husbands: Evelyn loves her wife so much she won't hear of her going into the trees. Such devotion, such selflessness.

Evelyn knows she isn't selfless. She knows she isn't brave. She knows that to lose Ada would be more than she could bear. Deep in the least generous corner of her heart, she is determined to be the one who dies first.

"The first day is always the hardest," says Ada when they wake before dawn on the morning the harvest begins. Evelyn nods. It isn't true, but they have to say it every year to get themselves past the inertia of dread. Tomorrow their hands will ache and their backs will cramp and they'll have to do it again.

It is cool in the still-dark when they leave the house, but not cool enough—Evelyn knows the day will be hot. They both wear heavy jeans, boots, long-sleeved shirts, and gloves. Ada's hair is cropped ruthlessly short, but Evelyn insists on wearing hers long, so she wraps a bandanna around her head. It is tied too tight and will make her head ache as the day goes on, but cutting her hair off would be conceding something that she can't define but knows she can't lose.

The worst part of harvesting is that the fruit does not want to be cut from the tree. The first fruit Evelyn drops into the basket hanging from her shoulder grows impossibly heavy and threatens to topple her to the ground. Evelyn holds onto the ladder and grits her teeth and squeezes her eyes shut and thinks she will die, but the feeling passes and the weight becomes bearable again. The fruits have short attention spans; if a ploy doesn't work quickly, they abandon it. Some of them grow fiendishly hot as Evelyn holds them steady and slashes their stems, but her gloves protect her from the worst of it.

She has cotton balls stuffed in her ears, in case the fruits begin to whisper, as they sometimes do—secrets, threats, or just an interminable tuneless humming that could drive a person to stick her knife through her own hand. One of the fruit's favorite tricks is to pretend to be a harvester and convince the person on the ladder that they are the fruit. The town loses a few that way every year.

Not everyone uses cotton: with her ears stuffed, Evelyn won't be able to hear Ada if she shouts from the ground to warn of danger. But they have a simple code worked out. Ada beats the lower rungs with her fists and Evelyn feels the vibrations in her feet. One strike means *look up,* two means *look behind you.* A ceaseless tattoo of bones on metal means *get to the ground, jump if you have to.* They've never yet had to use the last one.

It's slow work, but by the time Evelyn is ready to break for lunch, her basket is full. She carries it to the barn and sets it in the row outside with the others. No one ever sees the door open, but later all the full baskets will be inside.

She grabs an empty basket while Ada unpacks their lunch of sandwiches and carrots—they don't eat fruit this time of year. They walk half a mile in the hot sun back to where their truck is parked, and eat sitting in the back, saying little. It's cool and shady under the trees, but no one eats there.

Evelyn and Ada sit in silence for a minute or two when their food is gone. Finally, Evelyn takes a slow breath and reaches for Ada. They lace their fingers together, skin to skin for the first time in hours, and squeeze. Then they put their gloves on and go back to work.

———————————

At the end of the day, Evelyn soaks in a cool bathtub with a splash of lavender oil, a luxury she feels guilty for allowing herself but one she can't resist. She closes her eyes and tries to visualize the day's tension rinsing off her skin along with the sweat.

Ada comes in and sits on the edge of the tub. She showered half an hour ago and her short hair is already dry. She runs her fingers across Evelyn's forehead. Evelyn catches Ada's hand and kisses the inside of her wrist.

"Thank you for keeping me steady," she says. She is referring to the ladder and more. Evelyn has suggested, not just once, that they leave this horrible little town that doesn't even have a name, that can't even be found on a map, and go somewhere you can eat what you pick from the trees. Ada is the one who always talks her out of that idea. If they leave, what's to stop someone else doing the same? If one person abandons their duty in the orchard, why not an exodus? And then what? Fruit ripening on branches until it falls to the ground, rotting, fermenting, attracting insects who gorge themselves on the liqueur and—there is no imagining.

No one ever leaves. Harvesting is terrible. Not harvesting would be worse.

Evelyn tries not to think about it, tries not to imagine what their lives would be if they had been born somewhere else, if they were just two ordinary women in their ordinary home, tired from their ordinary work, about to fall asleep and dream ordinary dreams. She tries not to pretend they are those women as Ada leans over the bathtub and kisses her deeply, then pulls her to her feet and leads her, dripping, into the bedroom. Forgetting who she is and where she is makes remembering all the more painful. Evelyn reminds herself what waits for them tomorrow, even as her thighs are wrapped around Ada's waist, their bodies marking the sheets with lavender-scented silhouettes.

Later, Ada combs the tangles out of Evelyn's still-wet hair while Evelyn's sweat dries on her lips. "There's one good thing about not being able to get you pregnant," she jokes. Evelyn tries not to tense, but Ada must realize she doesn't find it funny, because she falls silent again.

Ada isn't wrong—they're probably two of the few people in town making love tonight. No one wants to find out what a baby conceived during the harvest might look like, or act like, or do. Even with every advantage of modern contraceptive care at their disposal, most women who aren't married to women just abstain until the trees in the orchard are bare again.

Natalie Milton didn't. Evelyn was only twelve or thirteen back then, Ada maybe ten, so neither of them have clear memories of when or how people realized that Natalie had stopped leaving her house. And they certainly weren't part of the group that went and banged on her door and refused to go away until she let them in, but they've heard about it so many times, know the story so well, they remember it like they were there.

The least-horrifying thing about Natalie, when she opened the door, was that she was visibly pregnant. Before they could process that, they had to take in the fact that she was naked and covered in soil—not filth, but rich brown dirt, packed an inch thick on every part of her body below the neck. Green grass poked through under her arms and between her legs. Evelyn always pictures an earthworm burrowing on Natalie's belly—she can't remember if someone told her that or if she just made it up.

"Can I offer you a drink?" Natalie asked politely. Someone pushed past her into the house and saw what looked like

Natalie's husband Michael, standing in a planter pot up to his knees, with vines growing around his body. Accounts differ on this point; some say the vines didn't just cover Michael, they came from him, sprouting from his eye sockets and under his fingernails.

Up to this point the story, and therefore Evelyn's and Ada's imagined memories, is very detailed. Now it starts to disintegrate. No one wants to talk about what happened next, about the screams and the sound of splintering wood that echoed up and down the street. Someone in the town must have been the last person to see Natalie Milton in one piece, but no one will admit it was them. And if anyone laid eyes on what was inside Natalie Milton, they haven't breathed a word of it.

So it's a good thing that Evelyn can't get pregnant with Ada. It's a blessing. Ada has said this so many times Evelyn feels she has no choice but to believe it.

"We could adopt," she said once, and only once. The look Ada gave her said without words everything Evelyn already knew about the unfairness, the cruelty, of taking a child from the outside world and bringing it into the inescapable shadow of the orchard.

They will go on like this. They will hold each other, and harvest the fruit, and eventually die, assured if nothing else that they have given the trees no new lives to devour. Evelyn lies awake, her arm growing stiff and tingly under Ada's weight, telling herself that will be enough.

Maybe it's the exhaustion after a sleepless night; maybe she is distracted, dreaming about the child she will never have. Whatever the reason, Evelyn's mind wanders for one crucial moment while reaching for a fruit, and a thorn stabs her in the arm. The trees never had thorns before, but that's no excuse for letting her guard down, she scolds herself, staring at where the three-inch spike of wood pierces straight through her flannel shirt into the soft crook of her elbow.

For the first moment, it doesn't hurt—all she feels is a pleasant sensation of warmth. Then the pain explodes up and down her arm, and Evelyn jerks backward and the thorn breaks from the branch, still lodged in her skin.

Evelyn screams. Her fingers are numb—she clutches convulsively at the fruit she was just about to pick. Its stem breaks, but it seems to roll from her fingertips faster than she can get a firm hold. What could happen flashes before her eyes as clearly as though she actually sees it: the red-black, fist-sized fruit plummeting to the ground, splitting open, leaking juice quickly absorbed by the thirsty soil. The horror of that vision eclipses the pain in her arm.

She lunges, one hand gripping the branch above her so hard her fingers ache, reaching with the other farther than she would have imagined possible. It's almost as if the fruit hangs in the air, waiting to fall, for one impossible sliver of a moment—just long enough for Evelyn to grab it in her fist and squeeze.

Through the cotton stuffing her ears, Evelyn hears Ada shouting from below. "I'm fine," she yells back, her own voice too large in the muffled silence inside her head. "I thought I was going to drop one, but I didn't." She doesn't mention the thorn.

The force with which Evelyn caught the fruit has crushed it. Inside the dark, gleaming skin, the juice is a startling shade of sunshine-yellow. It drips into the folds of Evelyn's leather glove. A smell rises from it, sweet and tart with just the slightest hint of bitterness, that makes her mouth water. She lifts her hand halfway to her lips before remembering that she must not, must never, taste the juice.

Evelyn's arm throbs where the thorn she almost forgot about is embedded. Wincing, she reaches behind her to put the mangled fruit in the basket on her back, then turns her attention to removing the thorn. Is there something else she should do first? She feels it like a name she can't quite remember, slipping away the more she tries to get a hold on it. The splintering end of the thorn rises from her skin like a bloody island from the sea. Evelyn pushes the skin around it apart with her gloved thumb and finger to get a better grip.

She holds her breath to steel herself against the pain, but the pain is suddenly gone. Evelyn's eyes widen as she stares down at her arm. A drop of golden juice, transferred from the tip of her finger, gleams in the wound, and Evelyn feels herself swell with an immense and beautiful feeling of peace. Everything in all the world is all right, or will be soon. She grasps the thorn and pulls. It comes out clean—when she looks back at her arm, there is neither pain nor blood, just a small, neat opening like an eyelid with no eye inside. Then that closes too, and the skin seals itself shut without a scab or a scar.

"How odd," Evelyn says out loud. She giggles at the sound; she's not sure she's ever said the words "How odd" before. She feels slightly intoxicated. It's a beautiful day. She tosses the thorn into her basket, and begins harvesting again, humming softly to herself.

Ada notices the rip in her shirt when they get home that night. "Did you get cut?" she asks urgently, peering at Evelyn's arm.

"It must have caught on a branch," Evelyn says with a shrug. "Probably when I thought I was going to drop that fruit and panicked. I didn't even notice it tearing."

Ada shakes her head. "We'll patch it up when we have a free minute, but wear something else until then. I don't like the idea of you climbing around up there with loose threads that could snag on…whatever." Evelyn imagines herself scaling the ladder naked, leaping acrobatically from branch to branch, juggling whole armfuls of fruit. It's funny, but she knows Ada won't think so, and she keeps the image to herself.

As soon as Evelyn reaches the top of the ladder the next day, she feels the cotton balls stuffed in her ears swell and expand.

What was soft silence a moment ago is suddenly agony, her ear canals stretched like overflowing grocery bags, about to tear.

Her heart squirms in her chest and her lungs deflate. Tears spring to her eyes. She's frantic as she claws at her ears, desperate to relieve the pressure. The cotton is growing, it's moving, the pain is unimaginable and she can feel it reaching tendrils into her brain, and she pulls, pulls, pulls, knowing that the cotton is alive and conscious, that it will tear her flesh and spill her blood before it will let go, but she doesn't care, no agony is too great if only she can get it out, and she pulls with all the strength she has.

Evelyn expects a fountain of blood as the cotton comes out, but all she finds in her hands is two spirals of wispy fluff, like clouds in a blue sky. The pain is gone and her head feels very clear. She doesn't put the cotton balls back into her ears, then or ever.

Every few minutes Ada sighs in her sleep. Evelyn watches her chest rise and fall with her slow, shallow breathing, and her own breasts ache. She can't stop thinking about what it would be like to nurse a child, to sleep with a small warm body curled between hers and Ada's.

When Ada rises in the morning, she finds Evelyn already sitting at the kitchen table, immersed in a pencil drawing in the margins of yesterday's newspaper. She's half-asleep and doodling more and more leaves on an enormous, overgrown tree, a child's tire swing hanging empty from its lowest branch.

Conversation helps the days go faster. Evelyn gets caught up in talking and the hours fly by, her arms barely tired from pulling and cutting and lifting. She doesn't know why she ever thought this was something to protect herself from. The trees are good listeners.

She tells them about the moment she first knew she was in love with Ada, how her heart simultaneously flourished and withered, knowing that opening her arms to this love would mean never being a mother. Until now, she had not admitted this even to herself, too ashamed to acknowledge that a fragment of her regrets loving Ada. Saying it out loud loosens a knot in her chest.

The trees tell her that it's all right. They comfort her. Leaves caress her tense neck and shoulders, whispering soothing things that aren't quite words. They tell her that she isn't wrong to mourn the children she will never have. That her sorrow does not betray her love.

You would have been a good mother, the fruit murmurs as she cuts it down. The words are soft vibrations through her palms.

You can still be a mother, the branches answer, rasping and dry.

Evelyn's hands keep moving, she keeps reaching for the heavy, slightly soft globes of fruit and piling them into her basket, but on a deeper level she has gone perfectly still. She waits, harvesting, yet not moving, for the trees to tell her more.

And they do. They tell her everything.

Evelyn waits until the trees say it's the right moment. The leaves arrange themselves around her, blocking Ada's view from the ground, shielding her from the gaze of harvesters elsewhere in the orchard. No one can see or hear her. It is a moment of pure, exhilarating freedom, but she knows it won't last, so she acts quickly.

She splits a fruit down the middle with her knife. It falls open in her palm, forming two perfect hemispheres. In the center of the one on the left is a knuckle-sized cluster of shiny green seeds.

Evelyn only needs one, but she takes two, just in case. Dark juice gleams on their hulls. Ceremonially, she places the seeds on her tongue and sucks the juice off. The roof of her mouth burns, then goes numb. She presses the two halves of the fruit back together, and they meld seamlessly, one drop of nectar on the tight skin the only sign that they were ever separated.

Evelyn drops the reunited fruit into her basket, then spits the two seeds into her palm. They look up at her like bright green eyes, like a child's eyes. Like hope.

Sitting on the edge of the tub with her legs spread, part of Evelyn hopes Ada will walk in. Maybe this should be a moment they share. It should be Ada's fingers, not her own, gently easing the seed inside of her.

But Ada doesn't come in, and in a moment it's done. Evelyn expected the same tingling numbness she felt when she held the seeds in her mouth, but it feels like almost nothing. Perhaps a twinge, like some infinitesimal tendril taking root in the dark and warm of her, but maybe it's her imagination. She wonders how she will know if it has worked.

Her mouth suddenly feels very wet. She leans over and spits into the bathtub and juice comes out.

———————

In the morning, Evelyn hasn't slept but doesn't feel tired. She watches Ada sleeping lightly in the early dark. Ada is so beautiful, so perfect, so ripe that Evelyn can't breathe. Impulsively, she leans over and kisses Ada hard on the lips.

Ada's eyes pop open. She doesn't kiss back or even move, aside from her eyelashes fluttering against Evelyn's. After a moment, Evelyn pulls away.

"You startled me," says Ada, rubbing the inside of her wrist against her mouth as though trying to wipe away a residue.

"I love you," says Evelyn. She can't think of anything else to say.

Ada is distant all day. Literally: the trees are taller than they've ever been, and the ladder reaches all the way to the top, hundreds of feet off the ground. It seems to have no more rungs than usual, but when Evelyn looks down she can't even see the top of Ada's head.

She has taken her gloves off and stuck them in her pockets. She likes the way the fruit feels against the skin of her hands, hot and velvety and so alive it's almost breathing. Lifting one perfectly round fruit to her nose, she breathes in the smell of copper and earth.

Congratulations, whispers the fruit.

———————

The harvest will end when the first snow falls. Evelyn doesn't need to look at the clouds to know it will be soon. She feels the blood slowing in her body as winter approaches.

Evelyn isn't showing yet, but she no longer has any doubt. She can feel the swelling of life inside her, a body that both is and is not her own. Her insides are moving, rearranging themselves to make room. Her stomach looks like it always has, but when she presses against it with her hand, she feels something rounded and harder than her flesh.

She wonders what her baby will look like. Perhaps it will have her brown eyes, or Ada's square jaw. There's no reason it should look like Ada, of course, but there's also no real reason it shouldn't. Perhaps the baby will be covered in leaves and bright spring flowers. Evelyn is excited to find out.

Harvest season, when the whole town works from daybreak to exhaustion and doesn't see a dollar, is always lean. Ada and Evelyn are used to stretching a pot of lentils to its breaking point, using their fingers to scoop the last broth from the bowl. It's a long, hungry few weeks, and they're always scrupulous about splitting meals exactly down the middle because neither can stand for the other to go hungrier than she must. But three mornings in a row, now, Evelyn leaves half her toast uneaten on the table.

It isn't because she's nauseated; there's no sign of morning sickness yet. She just doesn't seem to need it, like she doesn't seem to need sleep anymore, content to lie awake listening to Ada breathe. Sometimes she leans over Ada's mouth while she sleeps, not quite kissing her, just inhaling the air that escapes her slightly parted lips.

The only thing Evelyn craves besides the scent of Ada's breath is sunlight. The trees are happy to accommodate, rustling branches out of the way so she can stand at the top of her ladder drinking in the October warmth through her skin.

Every day that the harvest drags on, Ada seems more and more exhausted. Her skin is dry, her fingernails ragged, though Evelyn never sees her bite them. She falls asleep earlier, exchanging fewer words with Evelyn during their sparse free time.

She does not notice that Evelyn is blooming. There is still no visible change in the shape of her belly, but everything about her radiates fecundity. Evelyn's skin is dewy, her eyes bright. Her hair is thick and glossy. She is a burst of springtime in the cool of autumn. As Ada withdraws, Evelyn's heart reaches for her more and more, wanting to share the swoon of joy that carries her through her days. She wishes she could soothe the worried lines on Ada's brow.

If only Evelyn could tell Ada about the life growing inside her, she knows she would see Ada's beautiful face brighten again. But the words stick on her tongue, like fruit not yet ripe, not yet ready to fall.

A layer of yellow-gold dried leaves spreads itself like a blanket outside Ada and Evelyn's front door. There are no trees anywhere on their property. Ada clenches her jaw and walks through the yard as though every leaf crunching under her foot is a snapping spine.

Evelyn has started making a list of baby names. Last week, she took the antique brass letter opener from the drawer full of assorted junk in the kitchen and tucked it under her side of the mattress. At night, when she hears Ada's eyes flickering with sleep under her heavy lids, she pulls it out, enjoying the weight in her hand. Slowly and carefully, in almost perfect silence, she digs the pointed tip into her thigh.

It takes a long time to scratch perfectly formed letters into her flesh without making a sound, but Evelyn has all night.

From the bloodless cuts, she scrapes away damp shavings of wood that collect in a pile on the mattress beside her. Each morning she brushes them into her palm and drops them in the trash without Ada noticing.

In the bath, she runs her fingers over the carved lettering, occasionally finding splinters. The list unfurls downward from her hip: Aspen, Chrysanthemum, Leaf. She does not worry about the distinction between boys' names and girls' names. Those categories do not apply. Her baby will be all-encompassing, resplendent.

———

Evelyn hears the first snowflake hit the ground, and for the first time in weeks, she suddenly feels hunger. It's enormous, more than just an emptiness or a desire—it has sound and color; it tastes like metal. Forgetting to be quiet, she jumps out of bed and runs outside.

Ada finds her in the yard, on her hands and knees, digging with her bare hands in the hard earth. Wrapped in a sweater, Ada is still shivering, but Evelyn in her boxers and undershirt doesn't seem to feel the cold.

"What are you doing?" Ada means to shout it, but it emerges as a whisper. Nevertheless, Evelyn's head snaps up, her eyes huge and white. Soil outlines her mouth and tumbles down her chin.

"Oh, God, you startled me," she says. "Sorry, did I wake you?"

"What are you doing?" asks Ada again. She can't find any other words.

Evelyn cups her right hand and digs it down into the hole before her, brings it out heaped with dark, gleaming earth. She holds it out to Ada as if in explanation. "See, if you dig deep enough it's still warm."

Ada sees something many-legged scuttle across the dome of dirt in Evelyn's palm. She sees Evelyn lift her hand to her mouth. Unable to move, she closes her eyes, but the sound of gritty chewing and Evelyn's satisfied sigh is as clear as vision.

"Why?" Ada is going to cry, and perhaps also vomit, but all of that is still a long way in the future.

Impossibly, Evelyn laughs. "Pregnancy craving, I guess. I wasn't sure if I was going to get those."

Ada wonders how she is still standing upright when all the strength is gone from her body. "Pregnancy? You were…" She can't finish the sentence. Of course she suspected that there was someone else, as strange as Evelyn's been lately, discordantly happy and bubbling over with energy during the most arduous, miserable month of the year. Some part of her knew, but she hadn't let herself acknowledge that she knew, and now the only thing she can think of to do is crawl into the hole Evelyn is still digging and stay there forever.

"No!" Evelyn laughs again. Ada has always loved the sound of Evelyn's laugh, but tonight it is awful, like branches creaking under an ugly weight. "Jesus, no, Ada. Not ever." She licks earth from the forks between her fingers. "This is our baby. Yours and mine. With a little help from the trees."

And Ada discovers that there are worse things than unfaithfulness. There's the frantic joy in Evelyn's voice, her dirt-caked fingernails, and the sudden realization that what she thought was sweaty locks of hair stuck together is actually vines, vines tangled in Evelyn's hair, glossy and leafy and alive, vines growing from Evelyn's beautiful head, pushing through her skin, a Medusa parody in shades of green. There are worse things than losing her love, because now Evelyn is standing up, reaching toward her.

Ada knows from Evelyn's smile that it's no use, but she tries anyway. "Evelyn, whatever it is, it's not a baby," she says, her legs finally strong enough to take a step back so her wife's soiled fingers don't touch her. "You know that. You know what happens when people get pregnant during the harvest. We have to do something about this."

Evelyn sighs. "I know people won't understand, but I'm not showing much yet. We can keep hiding it a while longer and figure out what to say so no one will be scared."

"Hide it? No." Ada shakes her head so hard she's dizzy. "We have to get rid of it, Evie. There are doctors—"

The breeze rustles the vines framing Evelyn's face, but otherwise she is perfectly still. Ada takes another step back as Evelyn's smile slowly wilts.

"This is our baby, Ada," she says. "We're not getting rid of it. We need this."

"I don't," Ada says, and now she knows that she was wrong, she's not going to cry, this is so far beyond tears that she might never cry again. "All I needed was you."

Understanding blooms in Evelyn's eyes, and she reaches for Ada again, but she's too slow. Ada is already spinning on her toes, pivoting into a desperate leap through the still-open door and into the house. She slams the door shut behind her and hears Evelyn scrabbling at the knob.

All Ada needs is a few seconds. The house is small. Evelyn's knife, twelve inches long and gleaming in the near-darkness, sits naked on the kitchen counter. Ada grabs it just as Evelyn shoves the door open.

"Why are you being like this, Ada?" says Evelyn, but she hardly sounds like herself anymore. Her voice is the sound of things crawling under bark. "I love you. I want to be a mother with you." A green bud has sprouted from the center of her tongue.

"Sweetheart, please," Ada whispers. Her grasp on the knife is weak.

Evelyn smiles and takes a step forward. "Our baby, Ada. Just imagine. We'll knit little hats and sing it lullabies." She sways from side to side, crooning tunelessly, "Rockabye baby, in the treetop...."

Ada swings the knife.

Evelyn's hand comes up to block it before it can strike her chest. The blade sinks into her palm with the heavy thunk of an axe chopping wood. There is no blood. Ada tries to pull the knife back, but it won't come.

"Our baby," Evelyn snarls, and with her hand still impaled on her own knife, she embraces Ada. She seems to have too many arms, all thick and supple as stems, twisting around Ada's waist, her arms, her shoulders, caressing her hair. Evelyn pulls Ada into a kiss. Writhing, Ada bites down on Evelyn's lower lip, hard.

Something spills out of the cut into Ada's mouth, salty and hot as blood but sweeter, sharper, stinging like good whiskey. She only tastes the juice for a moment before her tongue goes warm, then numb. The feeling spreads down her throat and into her chest, and she grows still as Evelyn lets her go.

The world blurs in front of Ada's eyes. When she focuses again, she sees Evelyn holding out her hand, the one without the knife in it. A single seed rests in Evelyn's palm.

"Ours," says Evelyn, and Ada finally understands. She parts her lips like a flower opening to the sun.

STEVE TOASE

THE JAWS OF OUROBOROS

BROKEN

feathers slid out of pinioned songbirds in the hawthorn hedge above me, falling as rotted grey rain. The ditch was not the dirtiest place I'd hidden myself in my life, but it was by far the most unpleasant. I knelt on sun-faded crisp packets, crushing down festering fur and hollow bones that snapped as I shuffled around and tried to get comfortable.

Pasha rested forward on the ditch edge, staring through a set of night vision goggles into the field beyond. Grains of silt and clay clods smeared across his cheeks as they forced their way past, dragged upward and out of sight. Out of habit, I reached down and checked the drab-colored climbing rope around my waist, fingers tracing the knots like a rosary.

"Four other teams around the edge, and one in the fox covert on the far side of the stone circle," he said, not bothering to quieten his voice. Over the sound of sandstone grinding against sandstone we barely heard each other speak.

"Are you going for all of them?" I asked, leaning close.

He grinned, rubbing his face to smudge more dirt across his skin, and pulled out the machete from inside his jacket.

"Every single one."

He pushed himself out of the back of the hedge, using his rope to help him gain a solid footing on the convulsing soil.

The standing stones had always been teeth. We did not see the jaws until they started chewing the earth from under our feet and tires. From underneath our town. All across the country, the landscape was eating itself, the topsoil itself digested. If you stilled yourself and watched the fields for long enough it seemed the plough furrows themselves had been torn from the land. Branches, hay bales, empty fertilizer sacks, old farm machinery and dead sheep. Anything too immobile to resist the gnawing of the stone circles was ground to paste and swallowed down hollow, echoing throats. Some of the masticated substance leaked out, pressed between millstone grit incisors to dry on the exposed, sun-beaten rock. "White ambergris" was the popular name. For those brave enough to risk their lives collecting it from between the crushing orthostats, it was worth a lot of money. Feed a family for months. Much more than whale vomit. Our client's taste, however, was a little bit richer.

Pasha knew his work. I did not hear him slicing through the safety ropes of the rival collectors, fibers unwrapping like severed tendons as they were set free from the security of their horizontal tethers. He just slit the throats of the anchor men minding the ropes in the undergrowth, and tipped their unresisting bodies out onto the plough furrows.

It wasn't that I had a particular problem with killing, or that Pasha was better at taking lives. If necessary, I could be as efficient as him. The other part of the job—the collection—freaked him out. Me? I didn't mind getting up close to the crushing stones as they consumed the fields in which they stood. Maybe it was the relentless hunger that unnerved him. Too close to home. Saw too much of himself in the continuous grinding of those stone teeth.

Half an hour later he was sat next to me again with a black eye and cut across his face, rope tethered back around his waist.

"One of them put up a fight, but my knife was bigger than his," he said, and tapped the bloodstained wooden handle of the machete with a grin.

Next was the waiting game. Heavier objects like livestock, or dead bodies, got carried toward the stone circles quicker. Taking turns with the night vision goggles, we watched ten bodies tumble across the field, like enthusiastic crowd surfers carried by an aggressive audience. We listened to the sound change as sandstone crushed ribcages instead of soil and dead crops. We waited until the powdering of bone finished and the noise dulled back to a steady hum.

"You're up." Pasha said, patting me on the back. I nodded and rechecked my ropes, and checked them again, because you can't be too careful. I watched him roll a cigarette and light it, coal end glowing in the scratching twilight of the hedge, wondering, not for the first time, why I trusted him. Money. Money was the reason I trusted him. Money was the reason why I let such a cutthroat watch my back. Without me he got nothing.

I could have just let the tide of shifting dirt carry me to the stones, but that was uncontrolled, and slow. Instead, I dragged myself on all fours, using some of the momentum of the field to push off with each foot. Getting there was the easy bit.

Digging my steel toecaps into the constantly moving furrows I leant forward and scraped my fingers down the surface of the stones. White ambergris felt like congealed fat, peppered with splinters and grains of soil. I pushed my fingers deep into the paste trying not to gag at the smell. I'd only smelt it in two other places—abattoirs and battlefields. A mixture of fermented grass and warm, clotting blood. Bone splinters stuck to my skin. This was what we wanted. I opened the first canvas bag and wiped the mixture inside.

Working my way around the outside of the circle, the danger was the rope becoming snagged between the orthostats and severing, leaving nothing to drag myself to safety. Every couple of feet I checked the knots, checked the tension, and moved onto the next gap, trying not to think what might lie inside that stone mouth. What might be at the bottom of the throat. In the early days they tried sending men down. Experienced cavers. When they did not come back, they tried drones. There were rumors the operators never recovered from what they saw on their monitors. I tried not to listen to rumors. They slowed you down.

In an hour, I'd worked my way around one side, back to the center, then around the other, two full bags across my back. Two more tied to the rope.

Getting out was like walking up a down escalator. Several times I felt myself losing momentum. Several times I felt sure the churn of dirt would drag me like Pasha's victims between the stones, but over the next hour I made my way back to the hedge, landing exhausted in the ditch.

"How much?" Pasha said, turning on a torch and letting the beam scud across the haul.

"Four bags."

He shook his head.

"Doesn't seem much for ten people does it?"

"Not at all," I said, rested my head back against the branches behind me and closed my eyes.

―――――――――――

Even in the dark, the crane-like dragline was too large to comprehend. Over twenty-two stories tall, it looked as if a small city block had been dropped into the field. The boom stretched above overgrown hedges, immobile like a gallows pole.

We got out of the car and I opened the boot to take out the bags. Pasha locked up, not that there was anyone around to steal the thing. The air smelt of silicone grease and human sweat.

"That's just showing off," Pasha said, sounding more impressed than he meant to at the scale of the vast excavator. He grabbed two of the bags and I went to open the field-gate. Each cross piece had row upon row of small mammals nailed to it.

"What are those?" Pasha said, the note of disgust in his voice unexpected from a person who slit throats for petty change.

I knelt down for a closer look.

"Moles. Dozens of dead moles." I reached out and touched one, my finger brushing the desiccated skin of its paws. I wondered how many had ended up milled between the teeth of animated stone circles. Maybe these were the lucky ones.

All but the smallest draglines walked on feet, and this was one of the largest, balanced on hydraulic pontoons each the size of a small truck. Few had been converted into private fiefdoms though. Even this far from any megaliths, the ground rumbled with the constant, unyielding consumption. Maybe a walking fortress the size of small village was a good idea.

A curve of arc lights pinned us in place. We put the bags on the ground and waited for the reception committee. I had no doubt that beyond those lights there was enough firepower to blast us to bone meal.

We stayed still. Footsteps rattled down the outside of the dragline until five men stood in front of us. The bodyguard bruised us in their thorough search for weapons, found our knives and showed them to each other, laughed and handed them back. A sixth figure stepped out of the shadows and stretched out his hand.

Even by the standard of high-level drug dealers, Papa Yaga was pure evil, and the knowledge he'd personally requested to meet us made me very nervous. You survived in my industry by not being noticed. Mundane and average were the qualities for a long career. We'd been too good too quickly and we were now on the private property of one of the most dangerous men in the country.

"You're the team who have been so successful in harvesting high quality product for me?" He smiled, feldspar glittering in the greyed enamel of his teeth. So he was a user, too.

He was short, only up to my shoulder, and slender, wearing heavy tweeds, mud-caked, expensive hiking boots, with a shooting stick on a leather strap across his shoulder.

"We've been lucky," I said. Pasha normally left the talking to me. Not that he couldn't string a sentence together. He just never knew when to finish, his mouth finding more words than was good for the situation. I preferred to speak with precision and never for very long.

"In my experience, luck is something crafted with chisels and hammers. Your acquisition has been too good to be pure luck," Papa Yaga said. He walked forward and rested a hand on Pasha's arm, his other on mine. "Let's walk to my office, and inspect your latest crop."

I expected us to go inside the dragline, and when his men turned in the direction of the boom I felt sure we were going to get powdered into the plough soil. He felt me tense.

"Don't be so nervous all the time. You two are my golden egg-laying geese. My prize sows. My show-winning heifers. I have no intention of disposing of you just when you're making me so much money."

The bucket of the dragline was vast. We waited while one of Papa Yaga's men found a torch and led us inside.

The sheer scale started to sink in. The bucket was big enough to hold a large boardroom table, several bookcases and filing cabinets. The walls left bare metal, stained with rust and rain.

One of Papa Yaga's men wrenched down a heavy set of roller doors. We each pulled a chair up to the table and somewhere out of sight, a generator started. Above us, lights flickered like swallows. I glanced around the room. Cobbles and dirt accreted to the corners of the uppermost corners, making it more cave-like than industrial. Grains of soil shuddered loose with the dance of the generator, rattling and bouncing against the steel floor.

"Any questions before we start?" Papa Yaga said, sitting down opposite and folding his arms.

"What's with the moles?" Pasha said. I looked down at my hands and prayed to the shreds of god that might still notice me.

"Moles?" Papa Yaga tensed. Behind him two of his bodyguards reached under their donkey jackets.

"He means on the gate. The skins nailed to the field-gate," I said, glancing over at Pasha. He was oblivious, staring up at the lights.

"Oh those," Papa Yaga said, laughing. He leant across the table. "Because the neighbors get too fucking upset if I nail the flayed torsos of my victims up in the lanes where the tourists can see."

I glanced over at Pasha and just hoped he realized how close he was to getting us decapitated, golden eggs or no golden eggs.

"I'm joking. They've been there for years. Some old gamekeeper folklore. Meant to scare away the rest of the moles. Hasn't fucking worked."

"Would you like to test the product?" I said, lifting one of the canvas bags into the center of the table.

"Fee-fi-fo-fum," Papa Yaga said. Several of his men laughed. For a moment I was tempted to follow suit, but kept quiet.

"Fee-fi-fo-fum?" he continued. "I smell the blood of an Englishman? Grind his bones to make my bread?"

I shook my head. Clueless was better than cocky.

He pushed his hand inside the bag, pulling out a lump of the thick white paste. The smell was more subtle now, but still filled the room with the stench of wet hay and clotting. From the center, he dragged out a splinter of bone, a gobbet of muscle still attached.

"We call this Giant's Dough when we market it to clients. When it has the additions you work so hard to acquire. My little joke."

Dipping the bone back into the bag he came up with a strand of dirty white Giant's Dough, placed it in his mouth, and with the tip of his tongue rubbed it into his gums. The whites of his eyes turned autumn leaf russet, fading to the color of stagnant water and dirty syringes. Infected wounds and seeping sores.

I'd never watched anyone use normal white ambergris, never mind the stuff we collected. Drugs weren't my interest, apart from the money to be made from them. I had no idea how long the effect would last, and glanced across to Pasha who, with a sense of etiquette I'd not seen from him before, shrugged so small it might not have been noticed by any of the guards stood around us.

Something shifted within Papa Yaga, and his eyes returned to their previous grey color. He weighed the bag in his hand.

"How many went into this little mixture?"

"Ten," Pasha said. "Some still breathing, others not so much. Don't know if that makes a difference."

"Can't taste any as it unwraps inside you. Maybe the odd little gurgle of congealing blood around the edges, but I wouldn't be where I am today if I was put off by a little congealing blood."

"We don't know how much actually gets pushed out between the stones," I said quickly, making sure we didn't oversell ourselves.

"Of course," he said. "I know this isn't some Cordon Bleu recipe. More a one-pot, cook-it-all, see what comes out at the end."

"If you need more killing to improve the taste, I'm happy to do that for you. Fifteen, twenty. Makes no odds to me."

There was a manic energy in Pasha's voice. Looking back, I think that was the moment I decided to dissolve our partnership as soon as politic. Papa Yaga glanced over at me for a reaction. I distracted myself by lifting the other three bags onto the table.

"Canvas bags as requested, to avoid contamination," I said.

Papa Yaga turned and spoke to one of his men who left, ducking under the roller doors. We all sat in silence until he came back with a set of scales and placed them in the middle of the table.

I watched Pasha while they weighed the white ambergris, or Giant's Dough, or whatever they wanted to call the crushed paste of several acres of English countryside and ten corpses. He couldn't keep his eyes still, gaze flicking from the piles on the scales to Papa Yaga and his men. There was a hunger there that was going to get us killed if I wasn't careful. I did not want to die because of his appetites.

One of the men noted down the quantities, did some conversions on an old desktop calculator and showed the total to Papa Yaga, waiting for approval which came with a slight nod.

"Do we get to see how much you're paying us?" Pasha said. I reached into my pocket for my knife. Maybe if I slit his throat first I might get out myself.

"You worry too much," Papa Yaga said. "As before, you will be well compensated for your work. I know how specialist your skills are. No need to worry about me conning you. I can pay you a very good rate and still make myself a small fucking fortune. Don't worry about that, little killing man. Follow me."

Papa Yaga walked out first, back to us, his men dropping in behind. It took a few moments for my eyes to adapt to the darkness. Until then I followed the sound of his footsteps. We stopped by one of the pontoons, a narrow ladder built into the giant hydraulic foot.

"I don't like to bring currency outside until it's leaving my possession," he said by way of explanation.

He climbed first. I followed. I had the feeling if I let Pasha go next he would get some stupid idea he could take advantage of that turned back. From the top of the dragline's foot we climbed a second ladder, then a third.

I'm only guessing, but I'm pretty sure when the dragline was tearing millions of years of geology from open cast mines there was no need for a panoramic penthouse.

In the center was a small lounge. What wasn't covered in leather was coated in chrome. Two young, half-naked models, one male, one female, draped over a white leather sofa the size of a family car.

"Please, take a seat," Papa Yaga said. He nodded to one of his men who returned a few minutes later with a holdall. I glanced in the top. Stacks of 500 Euro notes bulged against the open zip. I caught Pasha's eye and got a gut feeling he was going to say something. I shook my head and hoped no one else noticed. Beside me, one of the models smirked.

"That all looks fine," I said, the need to be somewhere else getting more intense by the minute.

"Another delivery soon?" Papa Yaga said, the glow from the in-floor lighting glittering off his igneous teeth.

"As soon as we can. We try to not harvest the same stone circles too often. We need tragic accidents, not rumors. If there are rumors there won't be any product."

"Of course," Papa Yaga said. "But not too long. I have a lot of buyers waiting."

———

I spent three more nights with Pasha, on the edges of stone circles consuming the land, while he severed throats and ropes. Three seemed like a good number to put distance between the audience at the dragline, while still getting out before Pasha got me killed.

My instincts were right. Each time we went out he got more erratic. More unpredictable. I could tell his attention was elsewhere. If I'd have known where I'd have let the stones take him.

I went to see Papa Yaga in person, because he struck me as a man who believed in etiquette, and explained Pasha would be carrying on with a new partner. Explained I was retiring for family reasons.

"Families can be very problematic in our line of work," he said, and held out his hand. I moved to Hamburg where I had no family and knew no one.

———

They caught me in Munich six months later, grabbing me as I left a small goth club in Kultfabrik. Whatever they injected into my arm cascaded me through a thousand personal hells. It was a long time before I smelt dry ice without checking to see if my skin was being scalded from my face. Waking to find both arms dislocated was a relief.

It was dusk and I was halfway along the dragline boom, legs a meter above the ground, arms wrenched out of my sockets behind my back. All my weight hung on narrow bracelets of gristle eroded into my wrists. I gritted my teeth and tried to stay still.

"I really appreciated your honesty in coming to speak to me in person, even though you were lying about family. It was an understandable, and acceptable, lie."

Papa Yaga was below me, sitting on his shooting stick, his tweed jacket thrown across his shoulder.

"If I'd found out my partner was so much of a liability I would have lied for a solution. The better lie would have been: 'I'm sorry Papa Yaga. My partner had an unfortunate accident where he impaled himself on an iron spike, and as I'm too old in the tooth to work with another partner I wish to retire.' I'd have tried to persuade you. You would have reluctantly, but politely, declined, and we'd have parted ways to never cross paths again."

He grabbed my bare foot and massaged the arch with his fingers, a soothing sensation going up my leg.

"I knew you weren't retiring to look after family. You struck me as far too sensible to work for me and have any relatives. Your ex-colleague, it won't surprise you to find out, was not as bright. He decided to try and rip me off. Keep the Giant's Dough for himself and give me some white ambergris with cattle bone pushed in. As if I couldn't tell the difference. We caught his partner, some junkie amateur, and flayed the blistered skin from him over several days. Pasha must have got wind and ran. We had to pick up some cousin he stupidly visited a couple of months ago. The cousin didn't know anything."

Using my bare foot, Papa Yaga slowly spun me around until I faced the main body of the dragline. The figure was pinioned just below the pelvis, steel cable on one side, pulley wheel on the other. Precision-placed to prolong life. The early evening light was too faded to make out to many details. Even over the sound of my own torn tendons I heard the whimpering.

"It's rare theses day I have a reason to fire up this old darling. I felt finding your ex-colleague's colleague justified the cost in electricity."

The dragline came alive. Vibrations from the engine sent tears further into my tendons. I screamed despite myself. Above me, steel cable rattled against metal guides then started to move. The cousin was dragged further into the crush of the pulley, hoist ropes resisting the blockage.

Papa Yaga held me.

"Don't close your eyes or look away. I'll cut your eyelids off myself."

The air filled with the stench of friction, until momentum eroded through the cousin's pelvis. The two halves of torso tumbled into a patch of corn stubble, plumes of steam rose as the last of the body heat hit the cold air.

"If you're amiable, I would like you to track down your ex-colleague and give me the address. Then we really will never have to see each other again."

If this was a film I would have asked "And if I don't?" He'd have tortured me in increasingly inventive ways. It wasn't a film, and I had every intention of doing this last bit of dirty work for Papa Yaga. It wasn't like I had any lasting loyalty to Pasha.

Over the next few hours they gave me a few more scars, just to make sure I understood my place in the plan, but all the while they seemed almost apologetic.

Another syringe finished me off. When I woke I was in a nice, anonymous medical facility overlooking some rolling moorland. I was sure the purple heather was dancing and I couldn't help wondering where the nearest stone circle was, or how long it would be before the laminate-coated walls would be dragged to be crushed to splinters between the orthostat molars.

I don't know what worried me more. Papa Yaga suspending me until my shoulders tore out of their sockets, or paying for the best healthcare money could buy to patch me up before I did his hunting for him.

I lost track of how many days I spent in that private room. At some nod from the consultant, I was dressed in my own clothes, bundled into a van and dumped into the nearest town, a mobile in my pocket with a single phone number in the contacts.

Addicts are creatures of habit. Goes with the territory. Around other people Pasha was always too keen to impress to give any truths away. The truth was too mundane. He gave up trying with me a long time ago, and had slipped into his natural accent several times without realizing. Specific enough to identify his home town, if you paid attention. Other occasions he talked about a club night here, or a landmark there. Enough detail to confirm my suspicions.

The town was small and too many people knew each others' business for Pasha's whereabouts to stay hidden for long. He'd splashed around stolen cash to try and find a hiding place, and I splashed around my own to find him.

The squat was on the edge of town. A large house, insides gutted by fire. Recent enough for the stonework to be blackened with soot, and the air still thick enough with ash to stick in my throat. The people living there didn't notice. They didn't notice me. They didn't notice what week it was. A bit of bad air wasn't going to bother them.

I found Pasha in the basement. Seeing his silhouette I thought he was praying, knelt in the far corner, away from the worst of the leaking pipes dripping verdigris water into stinking pools on the stone flags. The damp made my wrists ache, and I rubbed the still-raw skin to ease the pain.

I thought about saying his name, but he was always faster than me. We were far beyond trust and loyalty now.

At first I thought the noise was a wasp nest in the room somewhere. The sound of constant chewing and tearing. I stilled my breath and listened. The grinding sounded too familiar. A memory of dead songbirds and decaying rubbish came back. I turned on the torch.

I don't know how much Giant's Dough Pasha had used. From the look of him I guessed we were talking kilos.

All his teeth had turned to stone, erupted vertically from his upturned face, and started grinding against each other. His skin was split by needle-thin rips. Inch by inch, fat and capillaries were dragged over the tiny menhirs and ground to paste. Around his neck wet muscle fibers were exposed, stretched taut as they too were dragged upward to be crushed and gnawed.

I shone the beam of light into Pasha's face. His eyes were open, staring straight up at the ceiling. Feldspar glittered in his pupils. Clear gelatin seeped over his mineralized jaws and down his torn cheeks.

Wrapping my jacket around my hand, I rolled up Pasha's trouser leg. Underneath all the dried blood it was impossible to tell where his ankle ended and the flagstones began. I dialed the number and waited for the call to connect.

Papa Yaga came into the basement by himself while his private army cleared the rest of the building.

I stood up from where I'd sat waiting on the damp steps.

"Weren't you worried it was a trap?"

He just smiled, and even in the dark I saw his teeth glitter. "Where is he?"

I took him over into the corner and turned the torch on Pasha, the chewing loud enough to drown out the sound of leaking pipes and footsteps on the floor above. He ran a finger over Pasha's face, collected a nail full of the pale gel and rubbed it into his gums. Reaching out, he steadied himself against the wall.

A woman came down the stairs, a Stihl saw in her gloved hands.

"You OK, Papa?" she said, looking at me and placing the saw on the basement floor.

"I'm fine. You won't need that. Call our land agent and have him buy this building. When you've done that, bring our guests from the holding cells. As many as you think this place can hold," he paused, and nodded toward the stairs. "Bring down those individuals you found in the rest of the house. Let's give them a purpose in life. Also, bring our entire stock of Giant's Dough down here."

"Everything is already on contract and packaged to go out," she said, still looking at me as if uncomfortable having this conversation in front of a witness. I knew I was uncomfortable being a witness to them having this conversation.

"Take samples of the white ambergris dribbling from that traitorous fuck in the corner, and get them out to our clients in the hour. First though make sure we have the deeds to this building."

The woman nodded and picked up the saw, leaving me alone in the cellar with Papa Yaga, and the constant sound of stone teeth grinding skin to paste.

"I'm sure you knew you weren't getting out of this room alive," Papa Yaga said, reaching out to take my hands in his. They felt warm and soft. Expensive. He massaged the back of my knuckles and leant in until his lips were against my ears. Peppermint on his breath stung my recently healed scars. "I hadn't decided whether to let my people take turns on you, or cut you up and feed you to our little crushing circle of stones in the corner. But considering the amount of money your ex-friend is going to make for me I'm giving you one chance to fucking run."

I looked at Pasha, now more self-consuming geology than man, and I did exactly what Papa Yaga suggested. I fucking ran.

ERIC J. GUIGNARD

THE FIRST ORDER OF WHALEYVILLE'S DIVINE BASILISK HANDLERS

I NEVER heard of basilisks 'til the night of Murrell's barn dance, but that was the night I met Rosalie, so the basilisks sorta took a back seat in my thoughts. I think it was Ronny Loom who told me, though his brother, Carter, was there too, and they're one 'n the same, being just a year apart and closer than spittin' twins.

"Poppa told me basilisks are crossing the Nolichucky River," Ronny said. "Heard Lilac and some men from Kingsport bagged half a dozen already, but more keep showing up. Lilac says they're worth more'n cougar pelts."

"That old trapper's still around?" I asked, more interested in hearing 'bout him than gabbing on new mountain game. Legend was, Lilac Zollinger had once been engaged to my great-granny Lizbeth, but Great-Grandpa Micajah dueled him for her hand and won, leaving Lilac with a bullet in the shoulder. He healed, except for his pride, which supposing got wounded the most. "Heard Lilac caught the scythe two summers ago by way of momma grizzly."

"He survived that," Carter said. "Thought everyone knew."

Me and the Looms passed under the banner for Murrell's dance and into his barn. Its double red doors were shuttered open and breathing yellow light like a hell cat, silhouetting straw-hatted farmers and their bonnet-hatted wives.

"Harv Ridout says Lilac won't sleep under a roof, but rather beds down amongst the trees each night so he won't soften up like us townies," Ronny said.

Carter added, "Harv Ridout says Lilac punched a wolf that was fightin' him over a cottontail."

I rolled my eyes. "Harv Ridout's got less sense—"

The sudden scream of fiddle severed my words, then the clang of guitar followed, and soon a gaggle of folks lined the varnished floor kickin' up their legs like a train of asses. I never cared much for dancing and don't know what others see in it. It's not like *kissin'* or anything, not even a little, and I should know 'cause I done both. Dancing, you're not even allowed to touch girls 'cept on their hands, or Pastor Wright'll whip your bottom scorched as Hell's eternal fury for such a sin.

That's when a girl I never seen before swung from the dance line, twirling delicate as a marigold bloom. Right away, my insides turned light and fizzy, like if ever I thought to float on moonlit mist, now would be the moment. She was tall and skinny, like me, but her hair went dark, and her eyes shone like copper pennies set in fire 'til they glowed and sizzled. She wore a dress pretty as first snow, and it clung to her in the middle and billowed out everywhere else as she moved.

Truth was, I never felt that way looking at a girl before, not even when kissing Aimee Greenwood last Harvest Day. I only kissed Aimee 'cause she started it, but I liked it too, though how it felt didn't compare a blue belle to how seeing this new girl weave and bow to each man in line did. Suddenly I felt dancing would be the greatest thing in the world, especially if with her.

"New girl in town," Ronny and Carter said together. "Heard her name is Rosalie Jacobs."

"Rosalie," I repeated, and I wondered where she came from. In Whaleyville, everyone knew everyone—even new folks—but she was a puzzler.

Murrell's barn was stuffy hot that night, and the back of my neck stuck to the shirt collar with sweat. I ran a checkered sleeve across my forehead and it came away damp and grimy, though I still felt my best in over two years, since that terrible day at the revival.

"I'm gonna ask her to dance," I vowed. But no sooner had the words been spoke did that vow fall to bitter ash when I saw Rosalie link arms with Luke Holder.

Ronny and Carter shook their heads somber as grave diggers. Luke Holder was older'n us, sized the three of us together, and meaner than a pecker full of sin. It was the cruel joke of the county that he was good looking too, with a big, perfect smile that made gals do funny things, and with eyes blue as winter quartz: cold and hard and sharp enough to cut, should you fall on 'em the wrong way.

"Hellfire," I muttered.

Rosalie and Luke swirled and dipped in the center of everyone, and Luke's hand dipped below her waist too, lower than was decent. I couldn't believe no one blinked at that, not even Pastor Wright, who would've had my hide skinned and burned for offering to His Heavenly Mercy. Rosalie giggled, and I could've puked.

"Heard Missus Janey's got sweet tarts she made from honeycomb," Carter offered as consolation.

"Sounds fine," I admitted, and we went off, the sounds of music and scuffin' all around, Joe Halverson's mouth harp pickin' up speed and Holly Barber calling steps.

Must've been forty, fifty people dancing in the barn that night, and the big oak beams shook with the ruckus of stomping feet and caterwauls and everyone-but-mine's laughter. We settled on a bench of hickory and tasted the sweet wonder of Missus Janey's tarts, and I started feeling better.

"Wonder if Lilac would take us with him after some of those basilisks," Ronny mused. "Wouldn't mind to mount one for Poppa's trophy room."

I shrugged my shoulders. "What's a basilisk anyway?"

"Ain't you heard?" Carter asked. "They've been crossing the Nolichucky."

"Yeah, I heard. What of it?"

"Well, they ain't natural. Jonas Teakle called 'em the kings of snakes, but said they're not entirely serpents either, only half-so. They were called forth by the pastor at Swannanoa's church, and he's to blame they're escaping, on account he's false and their church is awful wicked and full o' sin."

"Can't be worse than ours," I said, mocking.

Ronny and Carter both threw me strange glances, and I pretended to wipe away crumbs, hiding my face. They might've said something unkind next, but then trouble occurred. Seemed Luke Holder hankered for sweet tarts, too, and he wanted Rosalie to delight in their savor alongside him.

Each was panting and flushed from dancing when they came beside us.

"...and then I split three logs at the same time," Luke told her. "And Judge McClellan said he never seen anything like it."

"Three logs?" Rosalie repeated back, that coppery fire of her eyes seeming to burn brighter. "You'd have to be strong as an ox."

"Bet I am!" Luke answered. "And hungry as one. Wait 'til you try these tarts."

Missus Janey had stacked several dozen tarts upon a porcelain plate, and set that on a tub for folks to help themselves. You could now see the painted rose blooms and vine swirl whimsies covering the plate's face, 'cause most of the tarts had been taken off and eaten within the first hour, they tasted *that* good. In fact, only two sweet tarts remained, and Luke and Rosalie reached for them.

I can't help it, but sometimes there's a sore, vindictive part of me that resents others gettin' things I can't have. That little voice took to whispering: *It ain't fair Luke Holder gets to have the girl* and *the last of the tarts.*

My arm didn't seek counsel with my brain and seemed to shoot out on its own—I snatched the last two tarts from the plate and stuffed 'em both in my mouth.

"Oh, no," the Loom brothers said.

"What in thunderation?" Luke yelled. "Those were our tarts!"

I tried to smartly reply how his name wasn't written on them, but my mouth was so full of the honey-baked pastries when I spoke all that came out were chunks of sweet pie and sugar-berries spittin' into Luke's face and the front of his fringe-lined dress shirt.

"Oh, no," the Loom brothers repeated.

My face flushed at the realization of what I'd done, and what I knew would be given in return: I expected the color filling my cheeks was probably as crimson as Luke's own face, though I wasn't mistaking his reddening for any type of shame. I wanted to tell him it wasn't my fault, I just act without thinking sometimes, but my mouth was sticky, and I feared what else might come out. I raised my hands to him, fingers outstretched in surrender, and they were smeared by the guilt of delicious berries. He lifted fists that could split three logs at the same time…

I expected Luke to be angry, and I expected I'd be hit, and I expected the Loom brothers to stand idly aside. What I didn't expect was Rosalie's reaction.

She nodded at me, like we were akin in something, and when her copper eyes glinted, I wondered what terrible secret she knew.

Then Luke's fists arrived.

———

Next morning was Sunday, and no one in Whaleyville missed attending church, regardless how poorly or humiliated they felt, or how many bruisings their face took the evening before at hands of the town lout.

Breakfast weighed heavy in my guts when we packed the rough pews of Whaleyville's First Methodist Church of God Holiness, and that was not a good thing. Never a sermon passed that I wasn't compelled to rise and sit and rise again, jostled and shoved by gibbering neighbors, forced to my knees, yanked by my collar, and threatened with eternal brimstone by frothing Pastor Wright. My innards cringed at the thought, as did my quivering knees. I hated it, just hated it, and each week I thought I might water my trousers wonderin' if the Lord would again save me.

"Receive the genuine Holy Ghost fire!" Wright shouted. "Receive, because God loathes any man who keepeth sin in his heart. Receive!"

"Receive!" Pa and Ma and my little brothers and everyone else in the congregation shouted in kind.

"Don't question His will like a puppet of Cain, fill yourself with faith! Receive the Word of God!"

Pastor Wright was fat, and I don't mean overweight like the seams of his suit coat needed loosening, but he was so oversized he couldn't even wear a coat, and the Ladies Auxiliary had to sew special garments for him, cobblin' fabric gathered by collection plate. When Wright bellowed *The Good Word*, his chins shook back and forth like each was battling to be saved first, and his belly plummeted down and bounced back up like a supplicating heathen. Suppose gluttony wasn't so much a sin to him as it was a half-handed suggestion he could shrug off while suckin' down a couple wine-basted pheasants.

"Receive!" Wright shouted again, and we echoed it, and he rattled off a thousand Bible verses, and everyone swayed and repeated those verses by heart, and they cried tears and fell to their knees while doin' so, and a couple old ladies even fainted.

Before the revival, that would've been the culmination of our sermon, the wailing-and-gnashing-of-teeth response to satisfy any holy roller that he'd put the fear of Satan in our hearts and brought us begging for salvation.

But Wright wasn't like other pastors and, for him, our worship thus far was just stretching before a ball game.

Prior to the revival, we'd been Whaleyville's First Methodist Church, without the "of God Holiness" tacked on its end. Walt Brackenbury was pastor then, and he was a fine enough man, tough on Sundays, but friendly thereafter. Then Creighton Wright came challenging, and he brought his tests of "true" faithfulness: *The snakes.*

For Wright, it was simple enough to uncover nonbelievers by way of handling rattlesnakes: After all, God would shield those who led a Holy seasoned life. The snakes knew your heart, and if you were faithful, then by Grace you'd be saved, and the rest be damned.

Pastor Brackenbury must have been a charlatan, not living a genuine godly life, for he didn't survive that first test of purity, nor did any others who clung to Brackenbury's "flaccid" style of worship. Indeed, I thought myself faithful enough, but that hubris proved me as corrupt as Cain's puppets, for the snakes bit me too—and I nearly died that day.

I'd since been terrified that my failings would prove too indecent an abomination to be weekly forgiven. I wanted to live God's life, not from fear of damnation, but from fear of the serpents. I tried, but my flaws were known...

"Satan throws lies in our face, and you must throw back those lies! Armor yourself with the genuine Holy Ghost fire. Receive!"

Ronny and Carter stood in front of me, and they screamed with arms lifted to touch the rafters, "Receive!"

Jenny Teakle, cousin of Jonas, started convulsing and fell to the floor flopping like a fish pulled to the bank of the Nolichucky.

"She's received!" went the joyous cry.

Old Mrs. Kittenridge, filled with arthritis, leapt in the air like a fervent hare.

"She's received!"

Mary Ruth Barton started screaming, only they weren't just shrieks, but actual words, though I couldn't understand them, sounding like a duck quacking in Latin. Her rabid tongue hung from her mouth, and she jabbered away as the others cried, "She's received!"

Four boys each carried in a snake box to Wright, and the sound of rattles clawed at my senses, louder and louder, promising to finish what they began two years prior. The beading sweat like I'd had at Murrell's barn dance returned to my forehead, only now it turned cold, even though the church already felt hot enough to cook us all. Someone shrieked and another collapsed.

"Behold the agents of God!" Wright proclaimed, pulling out a rattler that must've been seven feet long. "Blessed be their judgment, for we will cast out the nonbelievers!"

That snake was a monster, hideous and terrible, striped orange and black with eyes yellow as angry flames. Wright held it to his huge face and the snake bared long fangs. "Jesus shield me!"

And he kissed the thing right on its awful mouth, a deeper kiss even than I gave Aimee Greenwood last Harvest Day, tongue and all.

"Only the repentant receive benediction!" the pastor shouted. "Come forth in faith!"

And we came: Pa and Ma pulling me in a rush with the crowd to prove none of them was less holy than any others, and I shook with terror.

The serpents were passed around like taking communion, people accepting and crying in tongues, and the snakes answering back. Parents and children caressed the rattlers together as if they were precious as a mewling infant's cheek, petting the sinewy coils and glittering scales. The crowd surged like a swirling whirlpool with Wright at its center, and his rattlers hissed and judged, and one-by-one the people of Whaleyville were found righteous, unless they weren't. Three people screamed for real and fell to the floor, filled not with His heavenly spirit, but rather filled with the wicked yellow venom of the vipers.

"Open your heart to the Lord, and repent your sins," Wright said, "or the snakes will know ye!"

Pa cried out, "I coveted my neighbor John Loom's crop of bean shoots last week!" and he took a snake.

Ma admitted, "I lied when I told my sons our dead dog went to heaven, since I know animals ain't got souls!" She took the snake passed over from Pa.

I was next, and Wright shouted, "Repent!"

Horrible thoughts of the revival tent came to me, two years back when I first took a snake. I hadn't been found worthy then, and a viper's bite sickened me with wither and seizures.

Memories brought terror, and I cried tears and shouted, "I had unclean thoughts about Rosalie Jacobs last night in bed!"

The shame washed over me, the stigma and guilt of everyone knowing my deficiencies. And suddenly I saw her, halfway back in the clutches of our shrieking and chanting flock, and I averted my eyes, but not before I saw Rosalie's red lips rise in a strange, biting smile.

But the power of salvation took hold and must have leeched the sin from my heart, for my mind cleared and I immediately felt righteous. I took the rattler by its neck and its mouth hissed open and a probing, forked tongue shot at me, testing, but I stayed strong, unflinching, even when its fangs reached for my wrist...

O! It rattled its war cry and tried my spirit, but finally acquiesced that my faith was good, and the serpent grew harmless as a spring pond.

"Hallelujah! Hallelujah!" went the cries, and I was proven righteous as the lot.

The congregation picnicked afterward, as the weather was fine, and folks gotta eat, so we may as well do it together since Whaleyville likes to call itself "tight-knit."

I still felt righteous, but I also knew I lied to myself a little, as part of me didn't regret at all those unclean thoughts of Rosalie...I only repented from fear of the snakes, which was greater than my desire of her, though that didn't cause my longing to be any lessened.

Gingham cloth was spread out, and some splintered benches and tables moved beneath giant boughed trees that were fat as Pastor Wright. The women set to laying plates and pouring drinks, and groups of men gossiped around us. I made out Herb Cranston's voice above the others.

"…Heard a basilisk got at Philemon Talbot's cousin in Kingsport last week, and that cousin died faster than a flying turd hits earth."

"We gotta do somethin' about it," said Holly Barber, who called the dance last night. Holly was a stout, zealous man with side whiskers that billowed under his chin like wild brambles. "Those snakes are crossin' the river."

"Ain't natural snakes, either. Hell spawn, called forth by Swannanoa's church. It's a wonder they ain't been struck down for the abomination they are."

"Snakes with the heads of chickens," Jonas Teakle added, winking at his cousin, Jenny. Jonas was always winking at her and, rumor was, he'd taken her in the husband-sense long ago and continued still, even though it wasn't allowed, them bein' cousins and all. He turned and winked in the other direction at another cousin, Jimmy.

Herb replied, indignant, "We oughta teach them what the holy judgment of rattlers can do…"

Other men joined in, and their voices and words became indistinguishable.

"You hear that?" I asked Ronny. "They're talking about snakes with chicken heads."

"That's what we were telling you last night. Don't you listen? And the basilisks ain't chicken-headed, they're rooster-headed."

"That's perplexing."

"Heard it true from George Templeton."

"Well, I never heard of such a thing." We sat squeezed between devout Jameson Lightspeed on one side and the freckled Peckingpaw sisters on the other. I thought briefly of the three folks snake-bit today, of what they might have done worse than the rest of us, then presumed God or Wright would either save 'em or damn 'em, and join us for chicken wings and slaw afterward.

Carter said, "Lilac's been trackin' the basilisks down, but the things ain't amiable to extermination."

Ronny added, "Heard you look at one and it'll turn you straight to stone."

I couldn't even reply, that notion sounded so asinine, and I made a face that told as such.

"And if the basilisks bite you," someone added from behind, "their venom will melt the flesh off your bones."

The voice startled me, being so near. I turned, and it was none other than Rosalie Jacobs.

I puckered with humiliation. No one wants a gal to publically discover she's the object of his midnight fantasies, and now I had to face her after professing all in church.

Ronny gulped. Carter sputtered, "A-Ain't heard that."

"I hear a lot of things," she said, "though just because it's preached, don't prove it true."

Rosalie stood over me as I sat, and her hip nudged my arm, and her hand squeezed my shoulder. The touch felt gentle and beguiling, a lush cloud to wrap me in scented billows. "That was brave," she said, "to reveal yourself like that."

"I—I'm sorry," I stammered. "I, *uh*...it just slipped out."

"You possess good qualities, Davey."

"You know my name?"

"Doesn't everyone know everyone around here?"

True enough. She still held my shoulder, and I saw the tips of delicate fingers splay toward my heart. Her skin was bronzed, and her nails white as daisy blades.

When I looked up to her face, all I could say was, "Where's Luke?"

Her red smile hinted that secret again from last night. "Luke has good qualities, too."

Naturally, I didn't know what that meant.

Carter brought the conversation back to him. "So what're you sayin'? Basilisks ain't real?"

"Oh, they're real all right," she replied. "Like your brother said, they've got the heads of roosters. And they have little wings midway up the body, stubby things like a baby bat. Not good for much, except lifting the serpent halfway off the ground."

Ronny said, "I gotta see one."

"So you shall," she murmured, and he looked at her curiously.

Carter got himself excited. "I heard they're born from an egg like a chicken, only it's the rooster that lays it, not the hen. You hear that, too?"

"A male laying eggs?" I asked. "That don't make sense. Has the basilisk got the plumbing of both sexes?"

"Actually, a male from any species may lay the eggs for basilisks," Rosalie answered.

My brain twisted on that, while Rosalie gave me a look that sent all wits leaping overboard. She continued, "Though basilisks themselves are always female."

And she stared into my eyes...

I heard in school one time that snakes on the other side of the world—cobras—can hypnotize their prey by staring deep into their eyes, and I thought of her look as that: I was immobile, transfixed, rent open for her to peer inside my soul, judging me, as did the rattlers.

Her gaze broke and she let go of my shoulder, shrugging a signal she was done with us.

"See you later, Davey," she said, and I knew that was a promise.

Rosalie walked away, though at the same time I could've sworn I saw her walking away also from Jonas Teakle, winking at him the way he winked at his kin.

———————

Next day, I woke to screams coming from the neighboring farm, and not at all like the rapturous screams during Pastor Wright's sermon. Pa took his shotgun and ran out, not even wearing a shirt. His bare chest was a carpet of thick black hair, whereas my chest sprouted but few hairs, and those light and scraggly at best.

He didn't wait for me, but I got my own rifle from the oak cabinet and ran after him, as it was my friends, Ronny and Carter's family, who neighbored us.

I arrived there and saw Mrs. Loom was a terrible mess, clenching and unclenching her fists like wringing out an invisible cloth. A pile of bones lay at her feet, pooled by stinking muck that breathed steam and bubbles. She looked like she wanted to touch it, but couldn't bring herself to do so.

Carter stood in the doorframe, pale as a bed sheet. He mouthed, "Oh no, oh no."

"Where's Ronny?" I asked, and Carter's tears told me exactly where he was.

I felt to collapse.

"Goddamned snake monster got in here," Mr. Loom roared. He carried a shotgun bigger'n Pa's. "It slipped out back by the coops. We gotta get it."

He and Pa went that way, and I followed, though they didn't care if I was there or not, so taken were they by hunter's bloodlust.

"Must've crossed from over the river," Mr. Loom yelled. "Damn that hellish town!"

I followed only halfway across the long yard, Mrs. Loom's cries nervously holding me back like a leash.

Just as Pa and Mr. Loom turned out of sight around the coops, I saw it.

The basilisk seemed to be waiting for me, poised behind a row of hedges, for only when I was alone did it pop out from the dewy leaves. A mask of feathered crust was the creature's face, and the red comb atop its head waggled like swaying sawgrass. Indeed, I'd heard it described, but that didn't lessen my shock seeing a snake with the head of a rooster. It wasn't big, maybe the length of my arm, and half of that was just a long, ropy tail, covered in jade-green scales. Its stumpy wings flapped like crazy, only strong enough to lift the serpent's upper body, just like Rosalie said, so the creature looked like a kite that isn't quite airborne yet, its tail still dragging the ground.

I raised the rifle, but too late, its eyes caught my own! I froze, remembering what Ronny said—*look at one and it'll turn you to stone.*

And it was true...I wasn't stone yet, but I couldn't move either, taken by the spell of its magic eyes, and I knew, just *knew*, the thing was reading me—the way Rosalie had—communicating something, or testing some quality of my spirit, and if I didn't pass, transformation of my likeness into rock would befall.

Its ancient eyes glinted at me, a wink of copper-hued acceptance, and I was released. The basilisk dropped tight to the ground, tucked in its lil' wings, and slithered back through the hedges.

I pointed my rifle under obligation and fired half-heartedly. My aim is terrible, and the bullet went wide, as I knew it would.

Pa and Mr. Loom came runnin'.

"I shot at it, but it got away."

Mr. Loom cursed and dashed toward the hedge, where I'd blasted.

I saw Pa glance, not after Mr. Loom, but the other way, enviously at a stand of golden peach trees, knowing that our own trees were withered and gave us shriveled and bitter fruit.

Pa caught my notice, sighed, and clapped me on the shoulder. "Good try, son. At least you tossed lead at it."

Ronny's death launched the town into arms-bearing fury. By late afternoon, a group of men gathered outside our church, led by Pastor Wright spittin' and frothin' and screamin' how we got to claim retribution, there being no allowance for serpents to kill folks in Whaleyville and get away with it (his own serpents being the exception, I presume).

The call went up for a party to hunt downriver next morning and kill every basilisk found, and then cross over to Swannanoa and see what needed doin' there.

Judge McClellan shouted agreement, and so too did Herb Cranston and George Templeton and all the others. Joe Halverson, who played the mouth harp, joined in, only he was smilin' all the while, though it was malicious-like, not a nice or secretive smile the way Rosalie gave to me.

"We oughta catch 'em alive and slice off their wings and tails and eyes, and send 'em still squirming back to Swannanoa's church," Joe said. He was known to break the legs of barking dogs just to watch them suffer for keeping him awake at night. Most folks felt righteous to avenge John Loom's son, but Joe Halverson was of a wrathful and vicious ilk, and he just liked cutting and torturing critters for any reason.

I felt uneasy going, but it's considered a queer thing in Whaleyville to ever decline a hunting trip. Plus Pa was big on it, and since I was friends with Ronny, everyone expected me to crave vengeance.

Though it's true Ronny was my friend, I didn't feel any obligation to avenge him; that small, resentful part of my brain reminded me neither of the Loom brothers ever defended or sought vengeance for me, even when Luke Holder practiced log splittin' techniques on my face at Murrell's barn dance.

Cold night fell, and it was all Pa could do not to wallop something, he was so excited and anxious about the basilisks, both killin' them tomorrow and double-checkin' every room to make sure they didn't slither inside tonight and get us first. Like me, he was temperamental, and I knew that small, resentful voice in my head sometimes also filled his own.

"The Looms have a stronger fence than us, and the creature *still* got through," Pa raged.

"The Looms thought they were better'n everyone else. That's what got 'em." Ma was wary of his moodiness, and weary, too, chasing after my brothers who were fightin' and hollerin' as always.

Pa kicked over a chair, shoutin' at no one. "Why should their peach trees and bean shoots grow more fertile than ours?"

It all seemed too much, and I decided I'd had enough and said so. "I'm turnin' in."

"'Night, Davey," they replied and went back to it.

I bedded down.

Outside, the moon was full like a pregger's belly, it glowing through my window, me pacified by its calm. I gazed upon it, letting sleep rise in slowly cresting waves, when a pebble *ticked* off the glass. The waves of sleep receded. Another pebble, another *tick*.

I went to the window and opened it, and saw fiery copper eyes lit upon a bright, pert face.

"How'd you know where I live?" I whispered.

"Doesn't everyone know everyone around here?" Rosalie replied.

True enough, I thought. *Except for you…*

She added, "I'm going for a stroll. Care to join?"

"Right now? At night?"

"Now is the time for all good things."

My mouth went dry. Quick as a whistle, I tossed on my trousers, shirt, and boots, and went out the window to join her.

She took my hand in her own, and it was like seizing a shooting star.

"Thought I'd head to Swannanoa," she said.

"That's fifty miles across the river! And what'd you want there, anyway?"

"There's shortcuts everywhere." Her voice fell somewhere between a whisper and a sigh. "And I'll tell you what I want…"

The road from my home was gravel and hard earth, but already it seemed to soften under my steps and grow dim beneath rising mist.

"Like to know a secret about your town leader?" she asked.

I acknowledged that I'd love to know Pastor Wright's secrets.

"Your pastor drugs the snakes," Rosalie said, enjoying my eagerness. "The vipers he keeps are harmless, much like a growling bull dog with no claws or teeth."

"Those rattlers got teeth aplenty," I countered. "I seen 'em, I been bit by one!"

"Yes, the snakes retain fangs, but their venom glands are removed. Only parishioners that need be taught his lessons are 'bit,' and sometimes unfortunate others, just to keep the rest of the congregation honest to him."

The perplexity on my face must've been obvious as a cannon blast.

She continued. "It's Creighton Wright himself who *bites* people. He's got a needle hidden up his sleeve that's double-pronged to match the width of snake teeth. It's filled with rattler juice, and he sticks folks while they're clambering around him, half-frenzied and clutching snakes, so it's not noticed he's the real culprit. People can rile themselves up as much as any rampaging spirit."

I thought of Wright and how large he was, wallowing in the center of us poor, teeming sinners who were unable to see from one side of his girth to the other. He could block our sight with one hamhock arm and we'd be none the wiser while he pricked someone.

"But why?"

"The usual cravings: power, ambition. Wright hails from Swannanoa, though he was cast out years ago, trying to supplant certain factions. He's a dwarf of a man with a giant's measure of himself."

"Go on."

She did. "Your former pastor was a faithful man, kept the river strong between our sides. And he died first at Wright's hand. Now the waters of the Nolichucky are shallowed to puddles."

And so it was, for I saw the once-mighty river far beneath us, a bare and cracked thing, winding between two worlds with no less impactful a boundary than a cobweb before charging steeds. Around us, the night shone brilliant, and flecks of gold and rubies twinkled in the sky, and planets and suns moved aside as we passed.

"You possess good qualities, Davey. Attributes I find attractive."

I blushed that she'd find anything attractive in me compared to Luke Holder. I asked, "And what're those?"

"Your imperfections."

I blanched. "Imperfections, like my flaws?"

"Aren't flaws what make men beautiful?"

"I'm not beautiful."

"You are to me," she said, and my heart filled my mouth.

We arrived in Swannanoa, and what I saw seemed nothing like Whaleyville, nothing like any town I'd ever known. Tall stone buildings crumbled at their tops, like towers long ago marred in siege. The walls were slick with dark lichen, their doors and windows mere openings rough-cut in masonry that showed distant fires burning within. The town slumbered in gloom as if being peered at through shadow wisps.

And it all swept by as a moving picture in fast motion.

Rosalie continued. "I have walked among you and chosen five whose qualities I love."

At this, my heart sank that I was not alone in her favor. "So you're sweet on five of us who are flawed? Wright must be the love of your life."

"Wright is too wound up in his own beliefs. He is wicked, yes, but not…obedient."

Rosalie's face was still of beauty, still of midnight longings, but I felt confused, beguiled, even with her arms linked around me, and we swirling though shadow wisps, the way I first saw her swirl at the barn dance.

And the sore, vindictive voice whispered in my mind, *Life ain't been fair since that revival…*

We arrived at the end of roads, the bedrock of dreams, the crossroads of light and dark. There was no signage, but I knew it was the fabled church we feuded with, the one Wright laid all blights: Swannanoa's First Church of Ecclesiastical Holiness.

And it seemed nothing like First Methodist Church of God Holiness. Whereas our church was a steepled box built of whitewashed wood planks, here a columned façade rose above the stars, and there was no door to close people out *or in*. A pair of stone basilisks stood at each side of the entry, and their eyes followed us as we moved inside where murky gloom wafted like the rest of Swannanoa.

And inside were more basilisks, and they came slithering to our feet.

"Wright binds you through fear," Rosalie said, her voice a slippery thing, like the serpents. "Here it is only love...love for the First Order of Whaleyville's Divine Basilisk Handlers."

"The what?" I said, feeling myself tense nervous, fearful, surrounded.

"They love those who love them," she replied. "For basilisks are not invulnerable. Like everything, there's ways to kill them, methods that are timeless, though not oft believed. Our congregation is growing, but still small, still weak. We need men of faith to help protect us."

"Truth of it, I ain't got much faith in anything."

"I will teach you faith. I will show you what it means..."

And when she kissed me, a plume of fire charged through my loins, and my eyes rolled back, and my heart slammed against my ribs like an untamable beast raging at its cell. My confusion, my fears melted away, and I gasped.

Rosalie's tongue prodded, slipped between my lips, entered me. It tasted hot and sweet as Missus Janey's tarts, as supple and smooth as butter cream warmed on the hearth. It was lush forests and flowered springs and misty sunbursts. And it was not like kissing Aimee Greenwood either...

Rosalie's tongue was slender, delicate, and longer than I imagined. Its tip split to a fork, and each end teased a place of my palate before slipping down the back of my throat. Her tongue filled my mouth, filled my airway, and still it kept sliding lower and lower like her hands as they plummeted below my belt.

My whole body went erect, and it seemed hard to relax and lie back on the stone floor when the whole of me wished to bellow in triumph and leap to the sun, but I let myself be led by the feel of Rosalie's blissful instructions, for she told me what to do without any words.

And the entire time, another little voice cried in my brain that this was wrong, this was a terrible, grievous calamity, and I must find the grace and strength to stop, *stop!* This was a different voice, unlike the mutters of resentment so often filling my head, but this new voice sounded mighty akin to the sermons of Pastor Wright, whom I hate, so I told it to shut the hell up.

Hell is exactly what this is, the voice replied, none too subtly, but by then me and Rosalie were as one, and nothing else mattered.

It was dark when I woke in bed, having slept not at all, and dawn when I arrived at the wooded banks of the Nolichucky, dreading what must be done: I gathered with Pa and the others to hunt down the basilisks.

Twenty or so Whaleyville men were there, though Wright wasn't among us. I doubt he even knew how to hunt, and his bulk would've given him a heart attack anyway, walkin' a quarter mile in those brambles. He was all talk in more ways than one.

I knew most of the others by sight: Philemon Talbot, Joe Halverson, Jameson Lightspeed, Luke Holder, Harv Ridout, Carter and his father, and a dozen more. Only one man I didn't recognize, and he moved among us with purpose and quick words, carrying a rifle and a pack made from 'coon pelts. Though I'd never met him, I'd heard more legends concerning Lilac Zollinger than any other superstition.

He was short and stumpy with a drawn, sallow face carved by hard lines like a mining expedition hacked across it looking for precious, pretty things, of which they found none. He was the oldest man I'd ever seen but he moved like a moonlit whisper, in fleeting darts and cloaked by shadow.

"You're Lizzie's kin," he said, eyeing me while ignoring Pa. "I can tell by the hook nose and way your shoulders slump. Always told her to keep her head high, but she didn't listen."

Took me a moment to figure he was talkin' about Great-Granny Lizbeth, who was granny to Ma.

"Didn't listen either when I said Micajah would do her wrong," the old trapper continued, though his loud voice fell quiet. "That duel 'tween us, my gun misfired. Should be my blood runnin' in your veins, not his. But tell her my regards still remain."

"She died before I was born, sir."

"That don't matter," Lilac shot back. "Don't matter t'all to tell her."

I didn't know how to reply, so cleared my throat in response. Some claimed Great-Granny Lizbeth died mid-life of a lingering sadness, while others said it was no more than Micajah's drunken fists. A fortnight later, Great-Grandpa Micajah got his throat mysteriously slit while sleeping in bed, and that was that.

"Ready to bag some basilisks?" Lilac asked to no one in particular. The other men grunted and hollered and raised their rifles in the air like a group of pale savages, he their elder chief.

"Whatever you do," Lilac said, "don't look in their eyes."

He unshouldered the 'coon pelt pack and pulled out small plates of reflective glass, explaining only, "Mirrors."

Holly Barber replied, "Pastor Wright said quotin' Old Testament scripture outta do the trick as well as anything else."

"Wright's got less sense than a filled crapper," Lilac snapped, passing out the small mirrors.

"What in Hades we need these for?" Curtis Merriweather asked. "Ain't gonna shave out here."

That got a laugh from the others who were in higher spirits than myself. Most treated the morning as a festive occasion like the annual buck tourney, wagers laid on who'd return home with the highest count.

"Use the mirrors," Lilac repeated. "Don't look in their eyes or you'll turn to stone."

———————

Curtis Merriweather was the first to look in their eyes and turn to stone. He let out an awful holler like a caught hen, knowing its head was about to elope at the nearest chopping block, and his flailing motions slowed, and his skin hardened to a cracked grey shell, and then Curtis froze solid. It didn't make sense at all, and yet there he was, become like the marble statue of Andrew Jackson that anchors our town proper.

Jameson Lightspeed was next to look into a basilisk's eye, and his cry sounded like a lark that's got its wing shot off, all high-pitched scrills and a fusillade of ruckus. George Templeton was a mauled bear, roaring and bellowing until he became silent.

"Don't look at their eyes!" Lilac reminded us by shouts.

Harv Ridout, like a jackass, followed Lilac's order by closing his own eyes. He stood there, rifle in hand, with eyelids clenched shut as if playing hide-and-seek, and a monstrous gold basilisk slid over, sinking its fangs into his foot. Harv screamed.

Lilac fired at the creature while it was vulnerable, pumping venom into Harv, and the serpent burst in half. Its body convulsed once and collapsed, while its winged rooster-head detached from Harv's foot, flew two flaps, then dropped to the scree with a gurgling *squawk*. Harv's skeleton fell next to it in a puddle, the venom having already melted flesh from his bones.

Several of the hunters surrendered their guns right there and fled for home, and maybe they were the smart ones.

"Use the mirrors!" Lilac ordered, and he shot another serpent.

After that, the remaining men sorta fell in line, 'cause the basilisks didn't get any more. Nonetheless, I can't say Whaleyville's men did much damage either, taking pot shots here 'n there, but at least by following Lilac's lead and using the mirrors, they avoided the serpents' gaze and even turned some of the basilisks' eyes back on themselves, which fossilized the beasts.

Lilac Zollinger proved a beast himself, a marauding archangel delivering bull's eye retribution through gunfire and mirror flash. He didn't miss a shot, and basilisk after basilisk froze to stone or blew to bits. It's a queer thing, gettin' in the way of a hurricane, and most of us ducked for cover, out of the line of his rampage.

And as I watched him move, victorious, indefatigable against that strange enemy, I thought of Lilac as being righteously triumphant, the sort of man we needed to lead Whaleyville, the sort of man—though gruff—who stood his ground for honor and justice and truly inspired faith. Here was a man who should never lose…yet in dueling for the hand of Great-Granny, he'd been jilted by a misfiring gun, and such are events that prove our fallibilities. No one can insure against all odds, no one can imagine *all* outcomes…

And surely Lilac did not imagine Luke Holder suddenly lifting a rifle to *him* and firing.

Lilac's forehead blossomed red, right 'tween his eyes, which bulged funny-big in surprise. It was a perfect shot and Lilac dropped like a load of grain. There wasn't anything Luke wasn't perfect at.

Carter mouthed, "Oh, no," just like he did when his brother got killed. I lifted my rifle and shot Carter also in the head, but of course my bullet somehow went askew, even though I stood only two feet away. His cheek blew in, and his temple blew out, though I aimed at his forehead like Luke had, but it was good enough regardless, and Carter fell beside the old trapper.

Joe Halverson shot Holly Barber, and Jonas Teakle shot Judge McClellan, and Pa shot Mr. Loom, declaring, "I never liked John Loom, anyway."

After the shootin', one other man was left over, Herb Cranston, who didn't know which hand to crap in. Luke levered in another cartridge and shot him, too.

That left just five of us, and together we lowered our guns, sharing in the moment.

Though I was with Rosalie all night, it seemed I wasn't the only one she'd bedded, for if I looked close enough at the other men I could see the slight matching bulges in their stomachs—like my own—marking the beginning signs of a basilisk egg growing inside.

Five remained, the First Order of Whaleyville's Divine Basilisk Handlers: Luke Holder, vain and mean; Joe Halverson, wrathful and vicious; Jonas Teakle, lustful and incestuous; Pa, petty and envious; and me, resentful and vindictive. Our weaknesses were known by Rosalie, and our weaknesses were loved.

Later, I'd wonder exactly how those eggs were supposed to come out, but there, on the way home, all I imagined was a fine and mighty revenge coming against fat Pastor Wright and his damned rattlesnakes.

ROMEY PETITE

PUMPKIN, DEAR

PROLOGUE

This is the twisted tale of Campbell Lot. Said to be haunted by a pair of tormented souls— two lovers who never found a way to be together in life. The ghosts of a woman named Lumina Pietrowsky and a man named Jack.

PART THE FIRST

Peter Piotrowsky could not explain his headless wife's return. He had buried Lumina's remains in the wee hours of that morning. She'd been in her silky white nightgown when the accident had occurred and that was what she'd been wearing when he laid her in the earth.

Last night, Peter had breathed a sigh of relief as he'd plunged the shovel into the rain soaked sodden Campbell Lot a final time. He'd stood then in the field where he grew his prize-winning pumpkins. A field he'd tilled for seven years. Six of those had been happy years. In the seventh one, things had come apart.

The following morning, Peter was awoken from restless tossing and turning by a knock, to discover Lumina's pale body upright standing on the wooden porch—covered in mud, nightgown ruined, fingernails raw, carrying one of Peter's prizewinning pumpkins under one arm, waiting for him at the door. Waiting for Peter to let her in.

"Lumina?" Peter gasped in disbelief.

Lumina's body did not nod. There was no head for it to nod with. Instead, it pushed past Peter, went inside, and upstairs for a change of clothes.

Peter had grown up a simple farmer. His mother and father had been dirt poor—raising fowl for eggs and pigs for slaughter and otherwise subsisting off turnips as they had in the Old Country. Little Peter—or Piotr—had seen many a strange sight while tending to his family's livestock. It was not unheard of that strange forces could propel the flesh long after other processes have died in the body. Only, Peter had never heard of it occurring in a human before.

He'd seen something like it happen with a chicken once. With his own two eyes. He'd been just a boy then—he'd seen it walk away from the chopping block—seen it walking around going about the rest of its day. Peter followed it around. It had taken three days for the body to die.

Love, too, is a bewitching force. To be in love is to feel mad desire to be one flesh. Not even the boundary of death can separate two souls meant to be.

Since coming home, Lumina's body had been nothing but sweet to Peter—the first thing it had done, in fact, was make him winter squash soup. Peter's favorite. As Lumina's body prepared the thick broth, it had used its own fingernails to cut a hole in the top of the pumpkin it had brought inside, taken off the cap with the stem—like a teapot lid and scooped out the stringy yellow pulp and seed with bare hands. Soon, the thick soup was ready and cooling on the table. Lumina's body hadn't made a bowl for herself, of course. She'd simply stood by, as if watching him. Peter sat down to eat, but after a minute was sorry to say he wasn't feeling very hungry.

After the shock of Lumina's return wore off, Peter realized he could not have her walking around this this—not as the chicken had done. Not that it was not fair to her memory—in her last year of life she'd really showed him the woman she had really been—no, he couldn't because it simply wasn't Christian. Eventually, she would be seen. If not by neighbors then by visiting family. She would become a local curiosity.

Questions would be asked. Searching for answers would lead straight back to Peter.

And yet...and yet, Lumina's body seemed to understand Peter's position in this. It had since remained in the house, always within his sight. Even now it was sitting silently, in clean modest clothes before the fireside, mending a suspender strap on the pair of Peter's overalls that had been torn by her nails in their fight the night previous—when the accident had occurred.

Peter knew for decency's sake he simply needed to cover up the raw stump. That would quell his beating conscience at least—the wound in his wife: he felt it watching him.

Peter had an idea then.

He picked up the scooped out hollow husk of pumpkin shell, turned it over and then set it over the stump atop the shoulders experimentally as if he were a ladies haberdasher or window-dresser fitting a display mannequin.

It was missing something.

It was then and only then that Peter remembered where he'd left the dirty carving knife. The storage shed's sink. That was also where Peter kept the unspeakable things he'd been hiding and working on—not pumpkins—but they would certainly have looked that way to any onlooker. Unless they looked inside.

In any case, he would have to leave Lumina to get it.

Peter told Lumina he would be back. He squeezed her hand and hoped she would understand this. He did not know how she still walked, much less how she avoided bumping into things, how she'd known to step up onto the porch or even thread a needle—her being without eyes or ears, but, for this reason, he trusted she would be there when he returned.

PART THE SECOND

Peter went out into his prizewinning pumpkin patch. It was where he raised his trophy winners. Each year at the State Fair he took home the award for bringing the largest, healthiest, most perfectly shaped pumpkin. A few years of this and Lumina's family—the Campbells—had been more than impressed both at the prize money and the profit he turned from his annual roadside sale. They were not impressed, however, with the couple's inability to produce an heir.

Peter continued to sell his pumpkins, year after year. Some bought his pumpkins for money, others traded whatever they had. He met all kinds there—even a man who called himself an alchemist. A man who said he knew the mysteries of life. A man with the scrap of paper containing information he'd traded to Peter—the young man being desperate for a solution for the one thing he couldn't seem to cultivate—no matter how he tried.

That had been almost—one year ago—when Peter was convinced his trouble had really begun.

In the afternoon light, a scarecrow lay violently battered by last night's storm—by something stronger than the wind. Its frame had been broken. Its head lay in the dust some feet away.

Peter's shed was a tiny, ramshackle, one-room house with a naked hanging bulb out it the field where the tools were kept. He trudged in muck-boots out to it across the field stopping before he got to it to peer down into an open pit where the dirt had been pushed away like a great big worm had wiggled, writhed, and crawled its way out of the ground. Peter's wife's body had unearthed itself from six feet down. What of Lumina's head—her real head—was it still down there? Why hadn't the body brought it up with the rest? Peter wondered. Why had it brought the pumpkin with it instead? Digging one's way out from so many tons of dirt, that would have taken some strength. Peter had heard of sheer feats of adrenaline performed in times of stress, a tractor lifted off a child's body perhaps, or someone taking the plunge to save another who'd fallen through the thin ice, but nothing like this. He wondered what else Lumina's body was capable of.

Inside the shack, pumpkins lined the dank, musty walls. Each day Peter checked on their progress. Opening them up to peer at what was growing inside. So far, he'd had no success with Stage One of the process, even with so many attempts. Because of that he hadn't even considered moving to Stage Two.

The carving knife was there in the sink where he'd left it. The blood was still on it. He carefully picked it up, turned it over, and inspected it. Why had he left it there? Did he doubt even for a second what had happened really had happened? That it was his wife's blood on the knife and his prints were all over the handle?

Peter knew a good person turned themselves into the police when they did something wrong—a smart person did not, because a smart person knows good people are stupid. That's what his father had told him, when Peter had, as a boy, visited his old man in prison. Peter didn't want not go to prison. His father had died there.

Peter couldn't read or write, but he was going to be smart about this. He knew from his mother that talking was how they'd gotten his father for bootlegging washtub vodka. Peter knew that the police only showed up to catch a bad guy, not listen to a story. Not about how a family needed money or how in their home country it had been traditional. That was how he had learned to keep quiet—explanations didn't mean anything or at least that they wouldn't save him.

Excuses are just stepping stones before someone accepted some harsh reality they couldn't yet fathom. Like a corpse that had unburied itself and was walking around. It was human to make up excuses—to rationalize a reason for why we should not have to be punished for our crimes. People are hardwired that way.

Peter had killed his wife, yes, but it wasn't fair. It was she who had been holding the knife when they'd been arguing. She was supposed to be chopping up winter squash for a warm soup. It had been a cold night. Both needed something warm for their bellies.

Instead, she'd cornered him with the knife and Peter, fearing for his life, had two options—to run or to—he picked up the carving knife. The very one she'd been using to—*Chop. Chop. Chop.*

He turned the valve and as mud-colored water burst forth from the toolshed's faucet. He waited until the steam was steady and clear before he began to wash it, running his fingers along the flat of the blade as the water splashed down to rewet and wash off the sticky, dried blood.

PART THE THIRD

Lumina's body had woken from her deep dream. Inside the body was the Will. The Will knew in life its name had been Lumina, because that was what the meek voice had called her. That was all it had taken—bits were coming back to her now. The Will remembered.

In her dream last night she'd been a tiny woman buried beneath the soil like a seed. She imagined herself bursting from her pod and beginning to grow and flower. As her head ballooned, swelling in size, she'd pushed through to the surface, and felt the sun on her limbs at last. She'd picked up a pumpkin and started for the house.

Without her head, Lumina's body could still see or you could call it seeing—which is to say the Will had some idea of her surroundings mostly from familiarity and repetition of navigating them. A kind of awareness floated just above the stump where what remained of her neck had been inserted into the hollow pumpkin. It floated like a light in the dark there. Lumina's hands reached up and felt its skin—the ridged grooves in the vegetable flesh of her new head.

She tried to lift her heavy head now and failed—instead having to content herself with merely turning it from side to side. It was dark, cave-like inside the pumpkinhead. She could feel her thoughts echoing around in the total blindness. She tried to speak, but discovered only silence. It was moist inside the pumpkinhead. It felt warm by the fire but Lumina wanted light—just as she had when she crawled out of the ground.

She'd awoken with a heavy head many times before, in life, but it had been one of a different kind—a hangover. Many a morning toward the end in her last year of life she'd awoken lying in the pumpkin patch after a night drinking with Jack. Perhaps that had been what she'd done last night—after all, she had no recollection of the night before.

It was then Lumina felt a hand squeeze hers. The large-yet-meek-man hand of her husband. Peter's. Only when he touched her could she remember her full name had been Lumina Piotrowsky.

Lumina Campbell Piotrowsky. That had been—was her full name. The name Piotrowsky, however, did not belong to her, she remembered. No. According to the law, she had belonged to it.

Lumina Campbell's family had once been poor Scots-Irish and had since patiently acquired and eventually come to own a lot of land. The Lumina Campbell's Lot, for example, was several dozen acres of flat grazing earth fenced in with post and rail to keep intruders out and horses in. It was in the middle of everywhere, but nothing was a short drive away. Horizontal beams of wood formed three-tier barriers then connected to the individual poles beaten at intervals into the ground. Besides that, it was some fields gone to seed, a few copses of trees, and a row of pines dividing property lines.

In those days a woman's true value to her husband wasn't her beauty; it was her what her father had to give to a potential suitor. Lumina had been blessed with both of those, but an enormous amount of debt as well. Though Lumina's family had nice things and had educated their daughters—they couldn't have fallen into financial decline at a worse time—having no sons to inherit or work their properties. The Campbell's could not care for their various acquisitions and had expected their daughters to marry men who would. For Lumina it meant the only man who would marry her would have to be willing to live in the middle of nowhere and undissuaded by the idea of getting his hands dirty. Peter was already accustomed to both. It was not an uncommon thing for poor men to marry up—transcending the class they'd been born into—their lives a Cinderella story. Lumina's family had given their house, their furnishings, and a mare. This ornate furniture was out of harmony with the modest accommodations of the Campbell cabin and made things cramped. Peter had brought little more than the shirt on his back, and could do little more than write his name, but he promised Lumina's family a return on their investment in him. All he needed was a year.

With a simple ceremony, Lumina and Peter Piotrowsky had been wed, and in that moment, her Lumina's husband became the owner of the several dozen acres of land that were supposedly her inheritance. The land was still called The Campbell Lot, but a Piotrowsky effectively owned the plot and was the decider of what was to be grown on it.

"Pumpkins," Peter said, "We're going to have a pumpkin patch."

"Why pumpkins?" Lumina said.

"Because they're easy to grow," was his answer and he gave his best attempt at a smile—seemingly to comfort her. A kind of determination radiated constantly from Peter. He wasn't educated, her father told her, but then again, he'd bothered to speak English and thus wasn't just another dumb Polack—not like the rest of his folks. Peter was determined to use what he knew to get ahead. It was probably why her father had taken a shine to him.

When she saw her family next, Lumina asked her mother for advice.

"What do you know about pumpkins?"

"They used to grow wild right out of our compost pile, dear. Like weeds. Don't you remember?" Mrs. Campbell said, tending to her roses with shears and garden gloves. A gramophone playing was playing nearby. Mrs. Campbell played music for her flowers.

Lumina did not remember. As a girl she'd cared little for chores and had an active imagination, much to her parents' dismay, Lumina had been unprepared for her family's sudden change in prospects. She'd spent little time in the garden—more on horseback or otherwise playing imaginary games with faerie folk in the woods distracting her from chores. She never imagined herself married to a poor farmer.

"They'll thrive, dear—really—all they need are the months of summer rain and sun to get fat—round and wide," her mother said, patting her daughter's belly.

Lumina could tell her mother wasn't just talking about pumpkins.

As far as her family was concerned, it seemed they were mostly glad to be rid of Lumina at last—she was to become the farmer's wife to have and to hold from that day forward, for better for worse, for richer for poorer, in sickness and in health, to love and to cherish, till death do they part.

Till death do they part.

Till death.

It hadn't been that way at first, not entirely bad, but after six years together, when Peter came in from his work in the field, he'd expected her to have his food made. When they went upstairs, he expected her to lie back with little in the way of coaxing or caresses and accept his seed. Then it was assumed she would to go to bed early with him, rise with the sun, and begin it all again.

Eventually, instead of joining Peter in bed at night Lumina sat up—awake. She roamed the house all hours. Then the fields of crops. Then the forest of pines. She went for restless night walks—and night rides on the mare. Peter never knew. She was always back in her bed by the morrow—at least, at first.

Peter rose early and gave her little so much as a nod and stare watching her from this—his prizewinning pumpkin patch. It was only then she began to resent him. How rigid he was.

This was the man to whom she'd been lawfully betrothed and wedded to. A man with dust-bowl eyes. Quiet Peter—who said very little even on the subject of growing things.

Warty-fingered Peter—his hands like a bumpy, gnarled gourd from having them in deep in manure. Peter the good, god-fearing Catholic—and yet, could not even read his copy of the Bible. Peter with his pumpkins. What was he doing with them? What was he up to in that shed?

Lumina had no clue—nor a key, but she'd found a page torn out of an old book once—sticking out of Peter's overalls. It was yellowed and folded up. She knew it couldn't be his, Peter never read and Lumina didn't know how else he'd come by it. She read over it and cringed, then again, then she put it back right away, her heart thudding in her chest as Peter came back from preparing for bed. From then on she suspected what Peter had been up to in the shed and wished that she hadn't. The thought of it kept her up at night—among other things.

PART THE FOURTH

It was while going for a night ride that Lumina had met Stingy Jack. Wry-mouthed Jack—handsome, but with a crooked smile. He tipped his hat to the lady on her high horse, patted the creature's nose, and asked her if she too was having trouble sleeping. Both like a gentleman and a link-boy, he offered to lead her and her horse and light the remainder of her way.

His name was Stingy Jack, but despite the name, Jack was anything but careful with money. His name, like everything else in Jack's life, was a joke. Jack spent every penny on the drink. Jack drank like a fish out of water, like a racehorse, like a drowned sailor, like an Irishman.

When he did have work, Jack claimed to have been a blacksmith. That was until he'd let his shop burn down to everything but the anvil and smoldering hearth. As he told it, that was why Jack had turned to drinking. To drown out his sorrows. Since then he'd "worked the corners" and played people's heartstrings, knowing all the old tricks for eliciting pity and when rejected, for acting the highwayman. He was a drifter, a grifter, and the rambling kind. He looked a little like he'd taken the hat coat and pants off a scarecrow.

There was one more thing about Jack. He had a lantern. Every night, he always had it with him. It glowed from within as Jack's eyes did—lighting their path as they walked through the woods on late summer nights. Every few nights, Jack and Lumina, night owls both, would rendezvous in secret.

As the harvest season approached Jack told her stories of how he'd tricked even the Devil into buying him a drink— on more than one occasion. How he'd taken the Devil by the horns and worked out a deal so he'd belonged neither to heaven nor hell. How he'd lived so long a time and yet, his body had refused to rot. He called it the Will.

Was Jack real? Lumina wondered. His hand felt warm in hers—it felt real.

When Peter awoke, Jack was nowhere to be found. He was always gone before daybreak. He took his lantern with him. And the rest of the bottle.

Peter said nothing of finding Lumina lying drunk under the scarecrow in the mornings that followed—he only continued to tend the farm and pumpkin patch by day, just as also he said nothing of the times Lumina disappeared into the night to go moon gandering with Jack. He simply did not speak of it. Nor did Lumina's affair with Jack end. Each dared the other to acknowledge what had happen and neither would.

Lucky Peter Piotrowsky, Jack had called him—because he had the most beautiful wife in all the land, and yet knew nothing about keeping a woman—showing a girl a good time. We could be rid of him, you know, Jack whispered in her ear. His snaggle-smile seeming to grow even wider. Lumina hushed him, reaching into his britches, taking hold of him and making his flesh grow in her hand. It too, felt warm and real.

Lumina knew Jack didn't want a woman. At least, not really. He'd been dead too long to care about a thing like that. He wanted a good, stiff drink. Still, a good stiff anything would take his mind off his weeping and troubles. When Jack wasn't too drunk he could still get hard. That was how she liked him.

There had been many nights in the pumpkin patch with Jack. On her back with her skirts around her waist. Her thighs around Jack's bony ribs. Her knees in the air, propped back on her elbows, and bare bottom in the dirt of the pumpkin patch. Jack burying himself inside her furrow—a ploughshare deep in a field allowed too long to lie fallow by the neglectful farmer. Lying on her back, Lumina could see the scarecrow watching them. She pretended it was Peter. A shovel was leaned against the pole that had been left out from earlier from when Peter's brow had been sweating—giving something for the thirsty ground to drink. Jack whispered unspeakable things in her ear as she sighed in his. How she could take the shovel now and use it to bludgeon sleeping Peter. How she and Jack might have lived happily ever after.

In the months that came, Jack talked more and more of being rid of Peter. He would set it up, but he always wanted for her to do it, for Lumina to deal the killing blow. Instead, she contented herself to closing her eyes and moaning over the Jack's shoulder,

"Oh Jack, oh Jack, oh Jack…"

It was then Lumina remembered with horror her last memory of Stingy Jack.

It had been raining that night. The rain had made it cold. Dirt in the pumpkin patch had turned to sloppy mud. The scarecrow was peering down at the three like a judge now—willing the executioner on. Peter had come out of the house shouting—calling to his wife, "Slut! Harlot! WHORE OF BABYLON!"

Lumina opened her eyes and looked up to see Jack hit Peter. Then Peter hit Jack. The two were fighting for their lives. First trading blows, then tumbling and rolling in the wet earth. Lumina all the while was shrieking at Jack, trying to warn him, "Watch out!" But it was too late, Peter got the shovel propped against the scarecrow. He swung it at Jack and caught him hard. Jack went down. Lumina screamed and winced from what she saw. Jack's face had been smashed. Now he was groping about in the mud, he seemed not to know what was still a part of his face and what was in the dirt. His jaw had been pulled from where nature had set it and hung bloodied now from a mouth limp and toothless. Peter struck again. Now part of his skull between his mouth and one eye were broken through—connected by a single fissure running up through both. Peter was standing over him. A moment later, the farmer's muddy boot caught him in the ribs. Lumina, fearing getting too close to the shovel, could only watch. Peter struck Jack again, red-faced and howling, "What has become of her? The Devil has taken her from me! WHAT HAS BECOME OF MY WIFE?" as streaming tears mixed with rain. All the while, Lumina could see Jack as he writhed less and less—a series of raw ends and irreparable damages trying to stand. Peter's shovel struck again, and with a shucking sound crushed Jack braincase, and his face into the earth—taking a great big chunk flesh and hair off with it. Jack was a mangled thing now. Death would be a mercy. Lumina closed her eyes as Peter brought the shovel down a final time. Severing her lover's head from the neck clean through. With his life, out went Jack's lantern and Lumina had fallen to the dirt wailing his name.

PART THE FIFTH

Lumina tried again to lift her heavy head and succeeded this time. She understood how this worked now. It had something to do with memory. Muscles could remember things. If the flesh had a memory the mind did not—could the Will, too?

Again then she sensed a presence in the room and felt the meek hand on that of her body. Peter's.

His other hand steadied itself on her shoulder then leaned in. She felt a point of pressure of the flesh of her pumpkin-head. Felt the steel knife slide through the husk. Peter began to carve.

A series of incisions were made. There were three triangles. Two big ones and one little one and a zigzaggedly longways mouth exposing the pallid flesh inside.

It was then that Lumina peered out from the angular eyes and raggedy mouth to see the familar setting of her living room and her husband in life holding the knife just as he had on the night when he'd lost his temper.

She was looking upon her husband, now. Peter. He had made her a face. It had a smile—it was sweet. He wanted her to be happy.

"Ah—that's so much better," Peter said, "Look," and handed her a mirror. Lumina did and agreed. She could see him now.

The pumpkinhead made it easier for Peter. Going back to the way things were. At last, he went to sit down and eat his soup. It had to be rewarmed, but Lumina was happy to do that for him. For the rest of the day she'd been all too happy to oblige him.

Peter still kept careful watch of Lumina. He didn't want her going for night walks or rides. Especially not with the pumpkinhead. As a consequence, the couple, man and pumpkinseed wife, spent more time together.

But there was a problem.

Had the priest not said husband and wife were to be of one flesh? Yes. Until death do they part. Until death.

And was there not a barrier that still separated the two? Had death not come between them? Lumina knew what she had to do.

She gave Peter not what he deserved but what he wanted one last time. She'd made him winter squash soup and that night, she lay back and let him fill her dead womb with his worthless seed. Then, as he came, in his wash of bliss, she reached up with her arms, took his sweaty forehead in one hand and his chin with the other and began to twist Peter's neck. In a split second came a crack signifying it was broken. Then, unsatisfied, Lumina's body finished the job by wrenching Peter's head clean off.

She looked at the body of her husband lying on the bed. His blood staining the white sheets. She thought of Jack.

Lumina was free. She'd done it—killed the bastard. She and Jack had talked about it for so long. She'd told Jack it was what she dreamed of—all she dreamed of.

Until now. She walked to the kitchen cupboard and put her pumpkinhead against one of the cabinet doors. She wanted to weep but she didn't have tears. She went to wash her dirty hands in the sink.

Then she went out to Peter's toolshed for a shovel.

PART THE SIXTH

Last night, Lumina had looked at her heap of rainsoaked clothing by the hearth. Peter, having freshly murdered her lover, was now stoking the fire. He'd stripped before it, changed into a spare pair of overalls, and begun hanging their clothes up to drip-dry.

Lumina was supposed to be making soup—a soup to keep them from catching death of cold. She stood next to the cast iron oven. It kept her warm.

Just like that all was supposed to be mended between them. Peter hadn't mentioned anything about Jack since he'd carried her indoors. All she could do now was stare at her reflection in the knife. Her hair was a wet mess. She shuttered and cringed.

"Peter?"

The carving knife was lying next to the cutting board next to which the process of slicing up a pumpkin lay unfinished. If Peter noticed, he made no indication. He was still staring at that fire. Staring right through it. His eyes like coals.

"Peter, we have to make a decision."

Peter, unresponsive, never answered her. He only picked up a stoker and began turning a log over and over in the fire.

"Peter?"

"I told you to make the soup…we'll catch a death of cold if we don't stay warm in this weather," he said and didn't say anything else.

"What are we going to do about Jack?"

Peter turned his head.

"What do you mean?"

"I'm talking about Jack. My—"

"Who is this Jack you keep talking about?" It came out before she could finish her sentence.

"What are we going to do about him?" Lumina said, trying desperately to make sense of things.

"What are you talking about?" Peter said, "There's no one out there."

"Jack. My lover. The man you found me with."

Peter looked at her bewildered.

"I'm talking about the man YOU MURDERED."

"There is no Jack," Peter said, and went back to stoking the flames, but he seemed to have more to say. After a bit, he did.

"For a time, I did think you had a lover. You left your bed at night. I followed you once or twice. You were just walking and talking to yourself. You wandered the fields, the path through the woods, but you were always back by morning. I began to think you were sleepwalking as some do, but then, you took the mare with you. Sometimes you took liquor along. I was so ashamed. My wife. Mad, drunk and rambling to herself like a vagabond."

"You can't just pretend this didn't happen. You murdered Jack. You attacked him with the shovel. You cut off his head."

You're mad, woman—I did no such thing."

"I found you lying in the pumpkin patch—lying in the mud like a hog or something worse—lying on your back there in the rain beneath the scarecrow. And what you were doing—you were—you were—"

"I was what?" Lumina said.

"That thing you were doing—touching—yourself in that way."

He wouldn't say it, so he said something else instead...

"An unwomanly thing. Wrong—ungodly—sinful. You've defiled our field."

"I've defiled my own family's field?"

"What kind of woman but a witch lies in the dirt like a pig and does such things?"

"You call me a witch? Don't think I don't have an idea of what you've been doing in that shed, Peter."

Peter looked at Lumina now.

"I saw found that page you had. The one you keep in your pocket."

Peter's eyes were wide.

"Where did you get it?"

Peter looked away ashamedly then back into the fire.

"You traded for it? Didn't you? A fool who gave his cow for a few magic beans. Can you even read what it says?"

"I don't need to. He explained it to me. I know what it says. The alchemist told me."

"Do you? What did he say?"

Peter had no response.

"I'll read it for you. If it hasn't been ruined by the rain."

Lumina went to Peter's wet hanging overalls and removed the scrap of parchment. It was damp in her hands. She shook it out, carefully unfolded it and read it to him.

"*That the sperm of a man be putrefied by itself in a sealed cucurbit for forty days...it will look somewhat like a man, but transparent, without a body. If, after this, it be fed wisely with the Arcanum of human blood, and be nourished for up to forty weeks, and be kept in the even heat of the horse's womb, a living human child grows there from, with all its members like another child, which is born of a woman, but much smaller.*"

There was a silence.

"You were trying to grow a baby—without me, weren't you?"

"The alchemist said he had seen it done. That anyone could do it."

"I don't know who sold you this or what they told you this was for, but it's not a human child. You were tricked."

Lumina felt such hatred for him. Watching Peter retreating into himself, just as his prick did as it had shriveled up—when cold, or emptied of its seed.

Peter stood looking at his feet. A silhouette against the roaring fire. Peter spent so much time trying to seem small—unimposing. But his shape couldn't hide now. At last Lumina could see her husband because he was blocking the light in the room. A big, dumb brute.

"You thought it was me—you thought I was the reason we couldn't bear a child. What have you been doing with those pumpkins?"

"I've tried everything in my power," Peter said, "Can you say the same?"

"And what have you made? A puddle of goo in a melon. What were you going to do next? Slaughter our mare? How far were you prepared to go with this?"

"What else would you have me do?"

"Have you ever considered the alternative?"

There was another silence. Peter wouldn't look at her. His eyes were wet.

Lumina walked up to the fire then and tossed the crushed scrap of parchment into it, then she went back into the kitchen.

"NO!" Peter shouted, trying to catch hold of it. He singed his hands only to discover it was too late. The paper went black at the corners, curled, then incinerated in the roaring flames.

Lumina looked into Peter's face lit by the glow. His dumb turnip face. She wanted to bury it in the ground.

"You killed Jack because he was a better man than you."

At last Peter turned and walked toward her.

"I killed no one," he said, looking at his feet still. "When I saw you, I lost my temper and in my anger I split the scarecrow instead of you. That is God's honest truth. Go see it."

"You're lying," Lumina said. She realized then she was still holding the knife.

"If you go out in the field now you'll find empty clothes and straw. Do you think I would just kill a man and leave a body lying around?"

"You're the one lying," she screamed, "You killed Jack!" But as Lumina said it, she knew it was true. She'd let her imaginary games get the better of her. Peter was right.

Lumina turned the carving knife toward Peter as he got closer—now it was pointing directly at him.

"My Jack needs a proper burial. If you call yourself a good Christian, you owe him that!"

In that moment, Peter's gaze met hers. The wind blew through his dust-bowl eyes.

"You won't deny my Jack a proper—"

"You are my wife..." Peter began.

In a flash, he had wrested the knife from her with his singed hands. "...and I am your husband," he said, forcing her down and pointing the blade back at her.

"Peter! Stop! You're hurting—" Lumina screamed, but found she could no longer speak. She could feel cold metal blocking her vocal cords from moving—even from coughing from the spittle she'd swallowed in surprise.

"You will never, ever, EVER THREATEN ME, AGAIN!" Peter screamed and seizing her by the lace-collar of her nightgown, forced it back into her neck—pushing her up against the cabinets. Lumina felt her head knock against the cabinet door. As it did she felt a kind of shockwave travel through her head and the object it had struck. She could feel the cabinet was hollow, yet hard, whereas her flesh—her life—was soft and fragile. She went for Peter's shoulder with her long nails. Digging her nails into his collarbone flesh. She heard fabric rip and seeing him face wince, but he did not let go.

Peter wanted to show her how it felt. To listen to her insanity. To be accused of so serious a crime by a woman who at times he believed belonged in bedlam. He wasn't looking at the blood running wild now—spraying from under her chin—to see how deep it had gone.

It was then he saw Lumina's neck was grinning at him from ear to ear.

"Jezu Kochany!" Peter howled, yanking his hand away, falling backward against the floorboards and making the Sign of the Cross.

Now the hot red was gushing down Lumina's nightgown—staining the white lace and silk a freshly-oxygenated sanguine.

He hadn't known his strength, Peter tried to tell himself. He could still get her to a doctor—yes, but then he remembered how far the town was from The Campbell Lot. That was when he had the nerve to look at last upon what he'd done.

Lumina sank to her knees—coughing and sputtering, bubbling from her neck and jugular, her head tilted forward then back as it had been severed nearly clean-through to her cervical spine.

"Lumina! My wife! My god, what have I done?" Peter cried and began to weep.

Lumina tried to tell him exactly what he had done but merely bubbled and frothed as her mouth made shapes. The vital fluid coming from her lips. Running down her chin.

"I'm going to jail now," Peter despaired aloud, burying his face in his bloodied hands. As much as he tried to practice saying, "She made me do this," he could not believe his words. Not with his heart.

PART THE SEVENTH
Lumina's body finished refilling the hole she'd put her husband down in and plunged the shovel satisfactorily into the field that was rightfully hers, but had been her husband's property by law. With her work done at last, she climbed into her own hole, and began to scoop and pull the pile of dirt over herself. Lumina intended to shed her old body before it started to rot. It would join her husband's in the ground where it might nourish the earth.

Pumpkins grow from a seed. In time, they change. Look at a pumpkin and its seed and you won't recognize the relationship unless you open one up and see the other. Vegetables take on an entirely different oblong shapes as the growing season takes them closer to harvest.

People don't change; they do grow, but that isn't quite the same thing. For as long as they live they'll always have the same roots. In life, there are things about them we can learn to forgive and perhaps, in time, even forget.

People don't really change until they die.

For one year, Lumina slept. Again she dreamed of being the tiny woman-seed in the ground. Once again, she grew toward the sun.

Next year, Lumina arose from the dirt. This time her head was a white ghostpumpkin the color of moonlight. She had become something new. Not a woman. Nor a pumpkin. But Lumina Pumpkinhead.

Her new body was an assembly of green limbs—a vegetable marionette that listed its fingers and obeyed the Will—a twist of tightly woven vines resembling human musculature wound together like sinew. The leaves made it difficult to stuff them into clothes, but she managed. Then she carved herself a face. There was no need for a candle to light her from within—the Will did that. How had her body reassembled itself—used the available materials to put themselves back together? It is a mystery. As was Jack's return.

Lumina welcomed a fellow Pumpkinhead among the new year's crop—risen as she did, from having nourished himself on bones. She carved him a face, too, gave him fresh clothes, and turned her back as he dressed—which was customary, even though with his body being made of vines as hers was he did not have reason to be modest anymore. The pumpkinhead man did not remember his name, or much about himself, so Lumina helped him—she told him his name had been Jack. He seemed to accept this.

"Now," she said, "We've slept for a year—we have a lot of work to do."

"Yes, pumpkin, dear," said Jack Pumpkinhead.

EPILOGUE Today, wild pumpkins still grow rampant on the abandoned Campbell Lot as the house mysteriously refuses to fall into disrepair. A neighbor man had taken to checking on the property sporadically but claims it mostly cares for itself. Once a year, he uses the grounds for an annual haunted hayride—it is a popular tourist attraction—as of this day the actual property remains unsold.

If Lumina and Jack indeed still walk the grounds, they've had the land to themselves for quite some time. What matters is the two are together at last. In the same flesh. It didn't matter what kind. Or who they had been before. They spoke in a different language now. A language without words. They haunted the grounds all but one day a year when they merely waved from their house to the children singing "Peter Peter Pumpkin Eater" on their hayride.

Lumina discovered new pleasures—gardening for one. Another was frightening distant relations who came to claim the property or teenagers who dared to trespass on her lot to do the kind of things teenagers did. Lastly, of course, she and Jack begin to experiment. How did one produce another Pumpkinhead without a body to nourish it? They were determined to find out.

Would Lumina and Jack have a family together at last? Come next harvest, they would have to see. Until then, they watched the garden grow.

STEPHANIE ELLIS

THE WAY
OF THE
MOTHER

JOHNNY Hedgerow slung his billhook over one shoulder, spun a mallet in his free hand and sauntered once more into the village of Cropsoe, the hub of the Weald. He walked the road with casual ownership, marched straight down the middle knowing no one would challenge him, every step establishing his claim. Wearing Hweol's livery, a patchwork greatcoat of emerald and jade, battered trousers shaded in earth and feet clad in boots of oak, he told the land he was here: servant and son, keeper of tradition.

Every year, he would return before the Wheel started turning to check the boundaries between this valley and the world beyond. Wood that had rotted needed to be stripped away and replaced with younger limbs, easily molded to weave the skeletal framework required to protect the land and the creatures who made their home there. Something told him this year the Weald would need more than his usual light maintenance. It had been a long time since he had carried out a Hedging. He licked his lips. Soon his blade would drink.

Only a few villagers were out and about, most busy working in the fields or hiding indoors. Mechanized and digitized modern-day life was kept at a distance and much that happened here demanded good, old-fashioned physical labor. The Wheel needed blood and sweat and occasionally tears to keep turning. Those abroad now stopped and stared, quickly averted their eyes should he catch them looking. Nobody acknowledged him directly, however. Johnny grinned. He had no hard feelings at such a cold reception; he was a servant of

Hweol as much as they were. Hweol, the one who turned, Hweol, the Wheel; *Hweol*, the circle of life.

Stepping into the bar of The Five Turns however, provoked a different reaction. Here the landlord and his wife were true Wheelborn. They were kin. They were family. Hweol's family. Blood spoke in this valley.

"Johnny, man," cried Simon, the landlord, pulling him into a bear hug. It was a meeting of giants. "Only when I see you do I know spring is here and winter well and truly laid to rest."

The two men smiled at each other, both fully aware of the meaning buried beneath. Winter had its own share of sacrifice and ritual.

"Brother." Liza came over and gave him a peck on the cheek.

Johnny gazed around. Being lunchtime, the bar was not busy but buzzed gently with friendly chatter and the clink of glasses. Oak beams and leaded windows, quarry tile flooring and low ceiling, the inn was a quintessentially English rural idyll. As he looked at them, these Cropsoe residents raised their tankards to him, met his eye. They too were Wheelborn, were family.

"A drink, sister," he said to Liza. "A drink to grease the oil that drives me."

He watched her take a tankard to a small keg kept separate to the large barrels supplying the pub's customers. This was a brew only the purest of the Wheelborn could drink. She handed him his pint and he held the honey-coloured ale up to the light. Deep and warm, it would remind him of what being a Wheelborn in this village meant, would renew the bonds between himself and every other inhabitant in the village, containing as it did, a contribution from all families there. Once he had emptied the cask, Johnny would know which saplings to cut down, where to start mending fences. Sometimes though, his family would tell him straight where the gaps in the boundary lay.

"High Ridge Farm," said Simon. "The world is seeping through."

"What evidence?" asked Johnny. Precise about his work, it was important to find the truth of the matter. To weave a false limb, an untruth, was to weaken the Weald beyond anything a mere gap could inflict. The drip of resentment, of the miscarriage of justice was poison to the Wheelborn. Until the time of ritual later in the year, the days of the Five Turns of the Wheel, when Hweol could claim whomever he wished, it was up to Johnny to nurture the veil between the worlds, to maintain the balance.

"The current," said Simon. "The air is charged wrongly in that house. I've not been able to pinpoint the source but it is there, somewhere."

"The Walkers," said Johnny. He knew them. He emptied his pint and wiped the froth from his mouth. It was time to go to work. In the Weald, the Wheel never stopped turning, Nature—always red, sharp-toothed and with jagged claws—pushed it ever onwards.

Johnny took up his tools and the bar fell silent. As one, they followed him out, formed the vanguard of Cropsoe's inhabitants. Others would attend the weaving, but not yet. First, the sapling had to be cut, new roots put down.

High Ridge Farm lay a mile from the village center, its land spreading from the house to the boundary of the Weald. It was one of the larger holdings in the valley. Homes were never built close to the border; Hweol did not permit it. So much was transmitted invisibly in the outer world—wireless messages assaulted their borders, digital images hovered in readiness to attack, a bombardment it was his duty to prevent. Cropsoe was permitted some things—limited telecommunications, basic television but not satellite, no internet, no mobile technology, no gaming. The restrictions were meant to protect the village, but occasionally a dissenter would declaim them as tyranny, smuggle in a mobile phone and snare the young of the village, even Wheelborn offspring. It was getting harder and harder to push back.

It took no time to reach the farm, the steady tramp of the Wheelborn alerting the patriarch inside to their approach.

He summoned his family and went out to greet them. Johnny stepped up to Lem Walker. They had known each other a long time. He had served Hweol well, observed the old ways, kept the traditions. Lem and his wife Anna had three children. Johnny sensed it was one of these responsible for the tear in the fabric between worlds. The young always wanted excitement, wanted to travel beyond, did not yet know fully the ways of Hweol. But which one?

"Come, children," said Johnny. "We will walk together a way. I have not crossed these fields for some time. You can reacquaint me with them."

"Child!" This from the youth.

Johnny looked at him. Karl. Nineteen and grown to manhood. How time had flown. Him? It would be a pity. A scuffing of boot on gravel from the lad next to him. Eyes as resentful as Karl's at the label applied—how old now? Seventeen? The third boy—no more than ten—just gazed on him with wonder. Hedging was usually a family matter and never discussed beyond their holdings. But the children were taught the ways and what was expected, should have been familiar with consequences. He raised his eyebrows at Lem.

"I told them of the ways," said Lem, understanding the look. "But they regard it as a fairy tale. My wife," he gestured at the small woman beside him, "did not want to frighten them."

Johnny turned his gaze on Anna. She had the decency to blush and lower her eyes. Had he left it so long memories were beginning to fade? In a way it was a compliment to his handiwork the boundaries had stood the test of time, the Weald had stood strong against the encroachment of the outside world. He laughed. If they were not frightened, they would come along easier. Where would the gap lie he wondered.

"Come," he ordered. The youths didn't move.

Lem pushed them forward. "You will do as he bids and walk the land with him. Perhaps you might finally learn a thing or two."

Anna opened her mouth as if to protest but the look on her husband's face stopped her.

"Consequences," growled Lem. "I warned you."

A mother protecting her children from the monsters under the bed, thought Johnny and he looked once more at the three boys. He could be generous. "You," Johnny said to the youngest. "You can stay with your mother."

The boy ran into her arms, sensing the danger charging the air around them. She held him tight.

"You two," said Johnny. "Now."

He turned and trudged across the field, not looking to see if the youths were following him. Knowing that they were. He was walking the path between the worlds and saw everything. It was time for the boys to meet Hweol. They left the Wheelborn behind with Lem and Anna. They would regather soon enough but for the time being it was just the three of them.

"So, you think me a fairy tale," said Johnny with a smile.

Karl shrugged, still defiant. "The stories are just meant to scare us, stop us moving away."

"And did they scare you."

Karl met his eye. The youth had guts, that was good, good for the strength of the weave. "No."

"And you?" Erik, he recalled.

This one looked less certain.

"The two of you have walked here often?" he continued.

They both nodded.

"What about here?"

Startled, the youths suddenly looked around them. They were no longer in the top field. They were walking the paths of the Otherworld. Erik moved closer to Karl, who finally began to look uncertain. The path was a wide forest track, bounded alongside by giant black yew trees, heavy boughs entangled with each other to form a dense canopy arching overhead. Only a dull grey light permeated through, gave their surroundings a hazy, surreal atmosphere. Johnny breathed easier here but knew for the youths it would be like walking underwater. The darkness of the trunks gave the appearance of a solid wall but if you looked carefully you could see some lighter shadows, tiny gaps allowing the inhabitants of this world to spy on their visitors.

"Where are we?" asked Karl, his eyes flicking nervously from side to side even as he tried to affect an air of unaffected casualness.

"I have pulled aside the veil between our worlds," said Johnny, "and now you see where the Wheelborn come from, the roots of your families. This is Hweol's realm. He is Nature's consort and it is she who has granted him ownership of the Weald."

There was a flash of silver between the trees, and another, and another. High-pitched voices giggled, their music breaking the silence. Imps come to see if they would be given a new playmate—their teeth sharpened especially for the purpose.

"I want to go home," whispered Erik, unable to tear his gaze away from one creature, bolder than the rest, who had stepped out of shadow and was shuffling towards them.

"Not yet," said Johnny. "You are expected. Look."

The track narrowed to a point beneath an arch of trees, their branches creating an awning draped with ivy, splashed with gold. A figure stood there, silent, majestic. As they neared, he heard Karl gasp as Hweol stepped forward to reveal himself. Stag's antlers protruded from the wolf's skull which crowned him, his robe was a bear pelt and his gloves, the moss of the forest carpet. Under his robe he wore clothes stitched from the tanned hides of creatures from both the Weald and this realm. His face was hidden so that those who looked upon him were unable to discern whether he was man or beast or forest. Nature had chosen Hweol for her husband and in him blood and sap mingled, the hybrid inheritance of the Wheelborn.

"These are the saplings," said Hweol as Johnny pushed the boys to their knees in front of him.

"One of them is," said Johnny, with a bow.

Hweol eyed them approvingly. "Good, sturdy stock," he said. "They will keep the Weald strong." He clamped Erik's jaw with his hand, jerked it up, forced the youth to meet his eyes, to stare into the skull's sockets and see him for what he was. Erik fought against his grip but Hweol was too strong. When he eventually released the lad and turned to Karl, Erik's bravado had vanished completely.

"They are both yours if you wish," said Johnny.

"It is tempting," said Hweol. "But we must be fair to the family and to the village…"

Johnny heard the regret in his voice. Hweol knew everything, knew who carried the guilt but he would leave their fate in Johnny's hands, allow the wheel of tradition to keep turning; a wheel within a wheel.

"You did not believe in me before," said Hweol to Karl. "Do you believe now?"

Karl's terror was palpable, no longer looked the man he was about to become, more the child he once was. He nodded.

"And you?"

"Yes," said Erik, his voice shaking.

"When you return, you will tell your friends what you have seen. You will describe me to them. You will tell them what I am capable of." And with that Hweol let out a howl. From the trees around him emerged his Hunters, one of whom dragged a man struggling and fighting before him.

"Uncle!" cried Karl. "How…"

The boys turned shocked faces to Johnny and Hweol before returning their attention to the man in front of them. A gesture from Johnny stopped them moving any nearer to him though.

"You thought your uncle had left the Weald," said Hweol. "I know it was he who fed you stories of the world beyond the Wheelborn lands, seeded the desire to follow him. I can read the minds of man, see their loyalty and their treason as clearly as if they'd spoken it aloud. He has been brought here for my judgment and you will witness his punishment. He cannot escape my justice."

Johnny studied the man he had previously delivered to Hweol. Martin, the boy's uncle, had become a sorry wretch.

Haggard and unshaven, clothes no more than rags, barely an ounce of flesh on him. He had been kept a servant in Hweol's court for a year—although such a year could be a lifetime for a man. Now he was good for nothing except as an example to his nephews. He whimpered at the feet of Hweol whose mossed hands gently raised him up as if to embrace him, then suddenly slipped around his throat and twisted with one sharp, swift movement. The snap echoed around the gathering. The only sound in the silence.

"Take him," said Hweol, tossing the body to his Hunters as if he were no more than a leaf. "He will feed the hounds."

Johnny watched the boys' faces. Now they understood the meaning of Hweol. That was one lesson learned. The next was to be his own.

"You can go," said Hweol to the boys who started to back away with expressions of relief. They thought themselves safe.

Johnny bowed to his father and followed the youths along the track. He let them lead the way, knowing the path would take them where he wanted them to go, not where they thought they were going and indeed when they emerged once more beneath the skies of the Weald, they were right by the boundary of High Ridge Farm. Beyond this was land not belonging to the Wheel and the village had to be protected from it.

Johnny walked up to the hedge. Parts of it were budding, small green shoots appearing to bring new growth, new life. He left that part alone, continued to walk its length until he came to a barren patch. Here the wood was dead. Almost. It still had a voice and it was time for Karl and Erik to hear it. A murmuring of voices drifted up to him, the Wheelborn had arrived. It was time.

He arced his billhook at the relic of rotting weave. The blade's edge whistled lightly above Karl's head, causing the boy to jump back. It carved through splintering wood which howled in protest at the attack. Johnny cut again and the growl developed into a scream, an unearthly wail of agony which sank its song into all who surrounded them. He sensed how much the youths wanted to run, but the Wheelborn formed a semicircle around them, a living fence of flesh to complement the boundary on their other side.

"Your first lesson," said Johnny, "is to cut out the old, strip out the rotten and corrupt."

Karl hesitantly reached out for the billhook. His face was white, eyes huge with the shock of recent events.

"No," said Johnny, gentling his voice, softening his message at the edges. "Rot breaks easily beneath muscle. You use your hands." He nodded towards the hedge and the boys stepped forward, glanced hesitantly at him and then proceeded to pull at the gnarled and hollow fibers. The Wheelborn remained silent but moved closer, intense observers, he heard their heartbeats combine and merge into one, form the drum, the rhythm, to which the boys' hands reluctantly kept time.

At first, wood came away easily and the boys made swift work of it, but eventually they came to a part that did not want to yield so easily. Again they looked to the billhook and again Johnny shook his head, although the way he raised the implement so that its edge glinted hungrily at them, caused the brothers to return to their work with renewed vigor and not a little fear. They tugged and pulled and tugged and pulled until their hands were ripped and bleeding. And still the wood refused to cede to their attempts.

"Now," said Johnny, nudging them aside with the tip of his blade and stepping in front. "Now we cut out the heart of the problem." He swung the blade down, heard the whistle of steel through the air and then a scream of such pain, the birds flew from their roosts and nearby sheep bolted. It went deeper than the previous screams, prodded at long-buried ancestral memory, told them of a suffering beyond experience.

"What was that?" Tears ran down Erik's face, his body shook, a damp patch appeared on his trousers. He started to call for his mother but stopped. Even in his shame he did not want to appear a little boy in front of the grown men surrounding him.

Johnny nodded his head with satisfaction, kept his voice soft. "A tear in the fabric, a soul of the Weald who weakened our barrier. He served his purpose and needs replacing."

Bewildered expressions remained on the boys' faces.

"I don't understand," said Karl, his terror not quite as palpable as Erik's, hidden better but still there. "A soul? Do you mean one of the village?"

"One of the land," corrected Johnny. He was a patient teacher and the lesson had only just begun. "Each family protects its own property with its own blood."

"But this is wood..." Karl picked up one of the discarded branches, felt its texture, ran his hands along the knots and stubs. As he did so, the surface flaked away and a whitish sheen shone through.

"They are more than that," said Johnny. "They are the limbs of your family. Branches rooted here sometimes for a century. This one however, has been here for a mere generation. It shows the blood in these parts is weakening." Johnny remembered this particular hedging. Lem's own father, the youths' grandfather. Another story they had not been told. In truth was protection, not in a mother's silence. Lem and Anna had got it so wrong, should have known better. He stared at the blade thoughtfully. Perhaps...

At that moment, he heard the quiet murmur of voices drifting up. Others from the village had gathered and were joining them for the hedging. Anna was not amongst them. "Go," he said to Erik. "Go and fetch your mother. Tell her she must attend."

Erik did not hesitate. He was learning. A good boy. Or perhaps he just wanted his mother.

Lem stood at the front of the group, a relieved expression on his face at the sight of both his sons even though this changed to one of concern when Erik ran past him.

"Family," said Johnny. "This is a time for family."

Lem moved up to the gap. "Have you decided?" he asked, his shaking hand snapping a piece of the discarded wood.

"Yes. We need to repair and reinforce. The weakness on this land has been building for too long. Your father and brother caused it and you allowed your sons to follow their path."

Lem rounded on him angrily. "I did no such thing. You took my father when I was a child. You forced me to witness his sentence. Do you think after seeing that, I wouldn't take heed of Hweol's laws?"

"Not consciously, perhaps," said Johnny. "But enough now to endanger us all. This land does not live by outside laws. We are left alone. And you prefer that, don't you? To be left alone?"

Johnny knew there would be no answer. They were all aware of what went on beyond their borders. Taxation, crime, poverty, war. None of that affected the people of the Weald. They were able to continue their lives autonomously, bound only by Nature's cycle. Almost an invisible world, outside minds slid over what they saw, blurred into nothing. But more and more Johnny sensed the pressure against their borders. External influences infiltrated the land via devices which shrank the globe to a cell, allowed instant communication. He could see the appeal to a younger generation, understood the need to explore but they were also needed here. Each generation served and turned the Wheel of Nature. If they left, if they were allowed to escape there would be nothing. Hweol would not permit that and nor would he. There was a movement amongst the crowd. It parted to allow Anna and Erik to make their way to the front.

Johnny stood quietly for a moment, took in the faces of everyone present, his gaze meeting the eyes of all. They were being noted, a census of a kind. They understood and remained respectfully silent.

"Sometimes it is necessary to re-establish the maternal bond with the land," he announced. "The mother is the bringer of life, the protector. It is she who wraps her arms around her family, defends them from attack." He took Anna's hand in his as he spoke. It felt small and soft but there was a firmness there and he could sense the strength running in her blood.

"You did what you had to," he said to her, "for your children. Do you regret any of it?"

The tiny woman—no more than a bird, really—seemed so fragile, an appearance belying the iron within. "No. If it meant I kept my sons from Hweol's influence that bit longer."

A mother's answer.

"Lem?"

Her husband stepped forward. "I disagreed with some things, but...I like a quiet life. Perhaps I am to blame for all this." He was standing up straight. "I have, and always will, serve Hweol. As the head of the family, I am the one who must be punished."

A father's—and a husband's—answer.

Out of all of them, Lem was the only one who truly knew what was to happen and he stepped forward willingly. But that was not enough. The land needed more than the young. This time it needed nurturing, a mother to look after it. Johnny shook his head. "A noble gesture," he said, "yet one I cannot accept."

The air shifted, shimmered so he could see the Otherworld wrap itself around them, saw the shadows of the woods and the path, the canopy beneath which Hweol still stood, his company of Hunters at his side. The Wheelborn saw them, too. Murmured and moved closer together. Such a gathering had not been seen for a long time. The hedging had taken on new importance.

"We gather," cried Johnny, still holding Anna's hand, "to renew weakened borders and protect our family. We gather to honor and protect the land that has fed us for centuries. The land needs its mother, is crying out for its mother..."

He tightened his grip on Anna as he detected the first flutterings of fear. He moved closer to the hedge, pulled her with him. "You protected your children," he said with a smile. "That shows you have strength. I was going to take one of them, as you knew when I arrived, but...I am a charitable man. I will take you in their stead. If you wish."

Now he could sense the terror rising in her, watched her turn toward her children, her husband. She had wrought this, even though others had started it. She had allowed the border to continue to weaken by her misguided actions. The consequences now were hers.

"I am Hweol's." She said eventually; there was nothing else. Her eyes had emptied and she no longer looked at any face beyond, was taking herself away into some small corner of her mind where she could separate herself from everything to come.

He was satisfied. She had good limbs, a mother's arms. He nodded at Lem, who lined his sons up in front of him.

"You must watch," said Lem, his voice shaking at first until his wife gave him one last look before she allowed herself to vanish completely. He rallied, his voice steady once more. "This is Hweol's will and you must learn it. Understand that and you will survive and live long."

"Mother!" All three sons called out to her, lambs bleating in the wilderness.

"You cry for your mother," said Johnny. "But there is no need. She will always be with you. You will watch and you will learn."

The world around them had dimmed and now all stood in the between place, the fine line between the real and the Other—although in the Weald who could tell which was which. The creatures of the Other moved closer, surrounded the Wheelborn, who watched only Johnny. He felt the pressure build, the sense of expectation rise, excitement in one world, dread in the other. Rarely was the hedging female. He moved the unresisting woman further into the gap, positioned her where she could be woven with the tendrils now reaching out to her.

First, he would capture her voice. The tip of his billhook sliced into her throat, and she sang out in pain. He withdrew the blade, let her sing a little longer, her ballad of blood nourishing the earth at her feet. And whilst she sang, three of the onlookers came forward and calmly dug a shallow trench around her. Into this bed Johnny lay the vocal chords when they were done singing and the eyes when they became sightless, the ears when they became deaf. Then the displaced soil was returned to its home and the hedging continued. His blade stripped cloth from flesh, flensed flesh from bone, the last becoming a reverential ceremony, religious and holy. Anna's blood carpeted the land and now Johnny honored the ivory of her, teasing out bone, gently pressing it into its new home, splicing wood and bone together so they united in a communion of sacrifice. First was the scapula bridge, woven into the height of the framework, then it was the turn of the arms, the sturdy humerus stretched to help the skeleton hang freely whilst he placed each bone. And against the backdrop of his work he could hear the sobbing of her children, the song of approval from Hweol. The boys thought him a murderer but soon their mother would speak to them once more and they would understand.

"Can't I take them home?" asked Lem, his voice choking.

"No," said Johnny without turning his head. "They must witness this. It is law. They have heard her sing one song, they must stay to hear her sing another. Sons must listen to their mother."

He heard a slight rustle as Lem retreated, still hushing his younger child and failing to still his weeping. Johnny turned back to his work. Gently he placed the skull between the feet. That would be gifted to Hweol. The mother would serve in both worlds.

Delicate carpal bones and phalange-tipped hands gripped unformed shoots, the rib cage opening up to embrace creepers already shyly approaching this newcomer to their home. Johnny continued to work respectfully, weaving a lattice between old and new, creating a trellis of skeleton and wood. Pubic bones formed a cradle in which life would once more be enveloped, a reformation of the womb. Femur and tibia provided a forked base, pushed into loosened soil, each nicked with the edge of his billhook to allow other saplings to graft and mesh with them. Young branches began to writhe and dance around the new framework, coating the body with a new dress, a robe provided by Nature herself. The whole hedge seemed to come alive as the last of Anna's bones were embedded and melded to the existing wood. A sigh ran around him, the pressure lightened. He could feel the strength return to this place of crossing. They had pushed back against the Outside and the Weald was safe once more.

Johnny glanced down at his hands, raw from his work and the cold, caked in dirt and sap and dried blood. He held them out to Anna's children. They moved forward, unwilling, but obedient.

"Come closer," he said. "Listen to wood and bone."

Closer still to the hedge they went, heard a gentle voice singing a lullaby, just as it had when they had been babes.

"She didn't suffer," he said softly. "And she isn't suffering now. Here she is still your mother, has become a mother to us all. You must tend this borderland. Feed it, nurture it. She is doing this for you. You must do this for her. Do you understand?"

Solemn expressions nodded at him. The grief etched on their faces tinged with acceptance and understanding. They would not leave the Weald. A tie had been made. This was the way of the land, the way of the Mother.

ZACHARY VON HOUSER

LEAVE
THE
NIGHT

THE nights hung in smoke and spilled drinks. The myriad of recollections and rotting futures fighting their way through the haze, those stagnant points like great pinnacles of ice hanging overhead, they couldn't get to him there. It was only in the blare of early mornings that things started to get bad again. Some stain on a coffee cup, or a hole in the wall, they would get their hooks in deep, they would split the blinds to let him know that they were still there. A restaurant passed would pummel him with a thousand pellets of reminiscence. The lines dragged into his mind held fast, the perpetual shiver in his gut nagged of what couldn't be fixed and what would never be built.

That first time, hunched over the counter with a thick coat of smoke on the inside of his mouth and a tear in his jeans, that was when a splash started to find its way into his coffee. It was just a little nip, *just enough to clear the head* he told himself, but how it grew. The night sky, out there with its cool breezes and softened lines, would feel eternally distant while those four half-walls penned him in, and he would put in a few drops more. Some old acquaintance, some face lost in the split that he most likely hadn't cared about anyway, would cross his path on a morning thick with evaporating dew, and he would need a big sip right from the bottle. But still, it was the physical things that drew him to those dangerous places the fastest, the most malignantly. That was when he pulled the bottle tightest.

He stuck to the places with the red light, they were the easiest to swim through. The easiest to trick himself away from the path in. The easiest to lose Laura in. He would rub at the grooved line that ran around his finger, and the red light would hide how pale the stripe still was. Three months after and he had only let it see the sun again two weeks earlier. Would the groove ever go away? Ten years is a long time. A lot of things change forever in less time than that. Someone lit a cigar at his side, a cheap stub of tobacco that always smelled like an old litter box to him, and his lit a cigarette. Life was full of little ways to hold back a tide.

Work was a problem, but at least it served as an occasional distraction. What the hell would he do with two weeks?

He tripped onto the landing where the stairs turned, and crawled a few steps before remembering where he was and pulling himself to his feet. Maybe he had had a drink too many a few drinks before. The slot shifted and danced before his key and he closed both eyes and took a breath before steeling himself enough to open one and try again. He choked the handle, locked his knees, and ground the key against metal until it hit the target.

"So, what are you going to do with your vacation?" Mark asked.

"Is that what we're calling it these days? Because I'm pretty sure that Tom said, 'Joe, I don't know what's going on but you're fucking up. Take a couple of weeks to get your head together and, when you get back, we'll take it from there.'"

"I mean, was he wrong?"

Joe put the mug down on Mark's table, Mark's mug on Mark's table. Like it or not, he couldn't, and shouldn't, forget that. He was a guest there until he could 'get back on his feet'.

"I...Shit, I don't know," Joe said. "I guess not."

"Can you use a coaster?" Mark said, and waited for him to slide one under. "So, what's your plan? You can't just mope around here until you can go back, worse off than when you started."

"Wait, I can't—"

"You know that's not what I meant. It's just that, *maybe,* just maybe, getting out of town for a bit might help. It *is* technically a paid vacation, why don't you treat it like one? Get something good out of it."

"I don't know, maybe I'll head back home for a bit."

"Thrill a minute, aren't ya?"

"Haven't been there in a while, and, well, I can't think of anywhere else."

"Whatever works for ya. When are you thinking of going?"

"No time like the present, huh?" Joe took a big gulp of coffee before setting it down to the side of the coaster.

"Tell your pop I said hi."

Joe went through the dresser in the little blue room that he was staying in. A dresser, bed, and a cramped, tiny table in the corner, that was all that he had but luckily that was all that would fit. Three pairs of jeans, four shirts, and a week of socks. He emptied the drawers into his bag, took a sip from the bottle of whiskey before wrapping it in one of the shirts, and zipped the bag shut. Glancing around, it was like no one lived there at all. It wasn't a room for living; it was one for waiting.

The air trembled with heat and motion as he left the darkened tunnel of the subway and stepped onto the sidewalk. Bundles of bodies in suits or t-shirts talked in a jumbled mess as they strolled or stood in the bus exhaust and honking cabs. Music blared from the endless strip of restaurants and shops, all competing to be the loudest, the most noticeable in a truly mediocre mob. It took Joe a minute to take it all in before his nerves calmed and he made his way towards the train. The constant, unrelenting assault on his senses whenever he was downtown, it had become a weight over the years. Did he really want to leave this, just to go to New York, the same thing on an infinitely grander scale?

The question was on a quick loop in his mind as the bell jangled. He took the short step up, and entered the train station coffee shop. It was all smells—coffee grounds, baked sweets, perfume, and wet dog—a consumer fog, all hot and damp. The woman in front of him took a step forward, and so came the quick, jostling sound of suit pants, briefcases, and light jackets like the false-starting of a worn-down steam train. An ancient man hobbled back, with the transparent hint of remnant hairs across his liver-spotted scalp, nudging between the tables as he made his tenuous way toward the door. Some dull jazz, or maybe something foreign that he didn't know, was playing at the head of the line. Calla lilies were fading to the same shade as the wallpaper's background, with buckshot thumbtack-holes scattered all through their delicate, spiraling petals. The espresso machine gave off a mean hiss and, for no real reason other than to have something to seem occupied by, he pulled one of the pins, took down the business card for a real estate agent, and pushed another hole into another flower.

Joe slid the card beneath his nail, cleaning the invisible grime that he knew hid somewhere deep and hoping that he would make his train, as a shadow fell over his hand and a new smell came to him. It was roses, and vanilla, and cool, vibrant growth somewhere far from man. He pulled his eyes up just in time to meet hers as she passed. They were green, but a green that he had never seen, like a mile-deep emerald, or some deep-lit sea from someplace with cleaner waters than he knew, flecked within that deep field, jagged slivers of crimson floated and seemed to glow in their brightness. Around her neck, a tight band of black and burnt orange was tied. She approached the corkboard by the door, pulled something from her bag, and pinned it into place.

There was a slight twinge of guilt, that second guardian that gave him a step-from-the-high-dive discomfort whenever he felt anything in another woman's stare. His morals had yet to read the divorce papers it seemed, didn't know that those guarded days had burned to ash. Some dance music, just memorable enough to leave a shadow through from the mid-nineties, was playing as he waited for his Americano. Water dripped from one calcium-coated tap and the creak-creak of one of the chairs was only rivaled by the sniffles of some summer cold. Joe dropped a dollar into the jar, pressed back through the crowd, and only just let his curiosity stop him before he made his way out onto the sidewalk. On the corkboard, alone save for a yellowed ad for guitar lessons, was one shining placard pinned and swaying from the corner. He slipped it into his pocket, rolled the thumbtack in his fingers, and replaced the real estate card with its bent corners.

VISIT HISTORIC BERNARD MILLS!

Rustic Life—Historic Tours
Seasonal Festivals—Family-Friendly Activities
Only minutes from beautiful Hammonton
and Cranberry Hill Observatory.
la Fête Faucon
Summer Festival | August 21st–23rd

GET AWAY AND BREATHE

He read and reread the lines as the train rolled on, his unused ticket to New York pressed between the pages of the paperback at his side. Through the grime-spattered windows, wooded backyards and suburban streets grew more sparse, chain-link fences replaced by rows of vegetation that raced toward the horizon, lawn mowers grew to mammoth, rust-blemished tractors. Weathered and burned backs arched over blueberry bushes, nimble fingers plucked and dropped, plucked and dropped. Joe pulled the bottle from his bag and took a hit as the intercom announced that they were approaching his stop.

He had nearly tasted the air before the train doors had opened and now, with the windows down as he pulled away from the car rental, it was nearly overwhelming. Damp leaves, cut grass, and the millions of pieces of ripe fruit in the surrounding farms enveloped him in a cocoon of luxury. He lit a cigarette and let his hand hover in the wind outside his window. The glimmering, steam-wafting fields seemed to wipe away everywhere that wasn't there from his mind, and peeking out from atop the trees, he could see his first destination.

His tires rumbled over the loose boards of the bridge, with Wading River, all copper-colored and foaming at the edges, gurgling below. In the distance, he could see a spot, just through a dense patch of trees, that seemed almost colorless. All greys that banished even the dullest tan or beige. The road of loose sugar-sand up to Cranberry Hill twisted and passed from patches of brilliant light to canopied twilight. *"The middle of nowhere couldn't even tell you how to get here,"* he thought while an old bus, full of dripping passengers and pulling rows of canoes, passed before he pulled down the single lane drive and into the parking lot.

The view from atop was startling. To be so high, and to see so far, without anything near to impeding his view, made him sit back a moment and stare at the floor. There was just an unbelievable carpet of green, the tops of tall trees, far below, and through binoculars, the sea at one far edge and the little blot of Philadelphia at the opposite. As his stomach settled, he dared another glance outward, though not quite so distant. Puffs of smoke, like white flags, trailed out from the green in little clusters. From a small, treeless tract, bordered on two sides by tendril rivers that converged on a pear-shaped lake, jutted out spokes of dirt roads or paths whose wavering lines he followed outward. The occasional twist around rock or river occurred, but nowhere could be seen an intersecting road from the outside world. A quick glimmer brought his eye back to the central point. There was nothing to it, just a pair of quick flashes, but something about the color seemed unnatural and, as he sat, it came again. He wondered if there was a town there that he could spend a day at.

"Of course," Joe said as he looked at his phone. "I can't even get a signal on the subway, how in the hell would I get one out here?"

There was a low rumble, like distant thunder, and he descended the long stretches of metal steps.

Joe turned up the radio and checked the map, the road, and then the map. How was anyone supposed to follow a map when none of the streets were marked? His binoculars bounced around the dashboard as he ran over the rocks strewn across the dirt road, the wind whistled through the window, map fluttering in his hand. He put a cigarette from the pack between his lips, wrestled with the map, and reached across the seat for his lighter when there was a pop and everything stopped.

He pulled his head back from the wheel. There was a dull, dead throb above his eye that beat with his heart, and where the seatbelt rested, the bone ached deep. The sun glimmered off of the spider-crack on the windshield where his bag had struck, and it took a moment before he registered the trickling sound where the whiskey ran from his bag, across the dashboard, and dripped onto the carpet below.

"Fuck."

The front tire of the car was sunk into sand up to the wheel well and an ugly wrinkle wormed its way up to the hood. A stuttering thump came from somewhere in the engine, but there was no way for him to discern where it was coming from. He wasn't going to fool himself.

His feet slipped from side to side in the soft sand, a trail of drips left in his stead, and some great bird circled overhead. He didn't know exactly where he was, but he guessed that it couldn't be far. It looked like the town had to be somewhere on that road and he had been going down it for a while, so all it would take was a bit of a hike. He lit a crooked cigarette, spat onto the sand, wiped his brow, and continued with only the foreign chatter of the woods as his company. In the distance, a light plume of smoke rose from the treetops and he aimed himself for that.

A few cigarettes later, and his mouth awfully dry, Joe came to a path that seemed to lead in just the direction that he needed. The bird still followed, but seemed to trail a bit farther behind. A drink and a seat, that was all that he wanted.

He cut down the winding path, the towering cedars and oaks dropping a cool shadow across his way. *A drink and a seat.* He leaned against a tree and took a break. A chipmunk darted nervously across the path, dodging between the holes that lined its sides. The sun broke through a passing cloud and something rustled the leaf blanket behind him. He smelled the heavy scent of roses and something sweet, but he couldn't place it. It was too hot, too damned hot. The lines of smoke were close though, so there wouldn't be long to go.

Above, wood carvings of birds of prey sat as sentries on the lower branches of the trees at his side, their grained eyes staring down at him like medieval gargoyles. He got the strange feeling that they waited for him, perched for that one moment when they would be granted life, granted the chance to take flight and rend the flesh from his bones. He brought his eyes down from the vicious watchers and saw someone in the distance, a young woman with her arm down one of the holes that lined the path.

"Hey!" he shouted.

She jerked her arm with a start, auburn hair flying in the wind, and bolted down the path and out of sight.

"Fucking weirdos," he said and continued toward the smoke.

The wooden hawks, owls, and eagles sat perched on their branches, watching the whole scene with predator eyes that would never blink, and continued on after he had passed.

His first step from the thin patch of woods between the path and town was like being transported through time, or at least to a place where the world had ended and a rebirth had begun. Small children ran past with clothes that seemed to have come from the 1920s and a woman pushed corks into dozens of milk bottles that sat in the bed of a pickup truck that rested, without wheels, on its frame. It was a bustling thoroughfare of dirt, all raw wood walls, buzzing conversation that he couldn't quite make out, and the uneven color of hand-dyed fabric. It swarmed, somewhere different than he had ever been, and churned somewhere deep in his brain. It was all so surreal, that cut from any reality that he had ever known.

"How are you doin'?" the man behind the bar asked as Joe stepped into the dim light of the inn. There was something foreign slid into his accent, just a light whisper of Europe.

"Alright. I was, umm, wondering if there were any rooms."

"Not a problem. We've got plenty left."

"Oh, that's great."

The old bottles of low-level booze sat over the bartender's shoulder, their vaporous depths calling to him.

"Can I get a shot of whiskey as well?"

"Double or single?"

"Double."

His room was unpainted wood from floor to ceiling, a large, four-poster bed sat in the far corner by a window. A small desk, barely more than the old desks from school, was placed by the other window. A large structure of brick and wood loomed from a few streets beyond, clearly visible over the short buildings that stood between it and his third-floor room, with loads of lumber being hauled toward it. Below him, the strange menagerie of archaic life strolled by.

"My car broke down a bit down the road, do you have a phone that I can use?" Joe asked.

"Sorry, we don't have one."

"I mean, I don't have to be the one that uses it, if it's for employees only."

"No, it's not that. We just don't have a telephone. No one in town does."

Joe turned toward him. They must take the whole *historically authentic* thing seriously, to an annoying extent.

"Well, I can't just leave it there..."

"'Course not. Some *produire* folks are going into town to sell off extra crops, I'll have them stop off and have it fixed."

"Thanks." He touched the lump on his forehead, pulling the hand down a drizzle of deep, dried red was noticed on the sleeve. "I guess there isn't a washing machine here, either?"

"Can't say there is. Can have some of the women do some wash for you, but it'll take a day or so."

"That's fine. Anywhere that I can buy a shirt until it's ready, then?"

The visitor's center looked like any other visitor's center in a historic place that he had ever been to, in that it looked like the rest of town. Old, wooden, dusty. The only things that stood out as modern were the glass cases which held maps of the area, collected local birds' nests, and ancient proclamations in French on yellow, cracked paper. Stuffed hawks and eagles stood on shellacked talons along the top of the wall, beaks dug into preserved snakes and rabbits. Past a little stand of Jew's harps and wooden fifes, cup and ball games and child-sized archery sets, he found a rack of shirts. With no marking of size and all in a similar shade of beige, he found the one that seemed most likely to fit, and brought it to the counter.

"Is there anything else that I can help you with?" the cashier asked after giving Joe his change.

"Yeah, do you know if there's a town around here?" He pointed to a point on the map, his best guess as to where the glimmer he had seen from the observation tower had come from. The path spokes were clear on the map.

"There's nothing there." The voice was colder now, authoritarian, the same European accent pushing through powerfully.

"I could have sworn that I had seen some shining, like glass, around there."

"It's just the ruins of a damned old glass factory and quarry. You'll find nothing good there. It's just a dangerous place." There was a pause and a softer touch returned. "There is plenty to enjoy here, anyway. We're just finishing preparations for *la Fête Faucon.*"

"Yeah, that was on a flyer that I saw. What's that all about?"

"It is a festival of the great…falcon. It is the, *merde, patron animal,* I guess you could say, of our town."

"And that starts tomorrow, right?"

"Yes. Tonight is a short celebration, of sorts, at the Great Hall but it is only for members of the community, unfortunately. Although, I'm sure that you will find the fête tomorrow unforgettable."

Out on the street, he lit a cigarette with the new shirt tucked under his arm, and across from him, he could see a group of women scrubbing laundry by hand with his bag sitting in the dust at their feet. Suddenly, as he watched them scrub, the thin stream of walking traffic parted and looked away. A quiet murmur rose, and a lone woman came quietly down the center of the street. She stood out like a flash, if only that her clothes were more vibrant, slightly more modern. Even with her head bowed, he could tell that she was also young, or at least young for her years, delicate-looking without the hard-worked wrinkles and strong hands of women he had seen thus far in town. He took a step into the street as she approached, and a barrel of wash-water was tipped into the street at her feet. The grimy liquid splashed over her shoes and left a line of mud up her shins.

"Fuck sakes," he said and walked over. "Are you alright?"

She tilted her head up to him and smiled, shining white teeth and the same brilliant emerald with crimson eyes as the girl from the coffee shop. He would have thought them one and the same, if it hadn't been for her much longer hair, all in big curls at the shoulders. Before he could think of anything to say, there was a shout from somewhere in the crowd and she hurried off, down through that patch of woods where he had entered town, and along the lonely dirt path.

A group of men, seated in the far corner of the inn's dining room, nodded as he passed through. The new shirt itched and, it was only once he had put it on that he noticed a similar golden V also embroidered on the shirts of the men that he passed. Though theirs tended to be noticeably weathered and vaguely faded. He rolled the sleeves halfway up his forearms beneath the licking sun, and left in a new direction through town.

It was far from a massive place, just a few square blocks made of trade shops and storefronts with the sounds and smells of living spaces cascading from open windows above. Crudely painted falcons, gripping lines of orange and black, stood in vibrant new coats of paint on posts and capped the sides of signage. The people that he passed were polite enough, but a strange formal distance was made well clear, and unending eye contact made him feel some sort of beast on viewing. He wished that he had a drink. It was so damned hot.

Upon turning the corner, he nearly fell back, a breath caught in his chest. His heart skipped a step and his cigarette fell to the mud at his feet. There, level with his eyes, was a grotesque winding and weaving of dried vines and wicker, into some vague form of a massive beak and face. Hunks of melted down, black glass made dead glimmering eyes, clumps of molted feathers were stitched into splotches on the bird's cheeks and were plastered into stretching wings and body behind.

He sidestepped the monstrosity, and came upon the great hall. A series of close, dark windows towered up along its length, with thin pillars of brick between, and from the branches of an old tree that stretched across the high roof some unrecognizable objects dangled from string. A group of children was clustered around a table in front of the windows, their shorts pulled tight at the bottom and hair outdated and long.

"Hey, mister!" one of them called. "We have Grand Faucons for sale."

"Yeah, you can't celebrate *Fête Faucon* without one!" Another sharp voice shouted from the group.

He crossed to the far side of the street and they rushed upon him, little hands pushing and pulling and demanding his attention for themselves alone.

"How much are they?" Joe asked, and from the swell of faces, he heard a dollar.

Well, that wasn't a bad price at all. He pulled out a bill, which was quickly pulled away, something brittle and tickling was shoved into his hand and they hurried back to their table. Glancing down, he some a miniature, even more crude version of the wicker and feather bird that waited across the street. Soiled down was adhered to twigs and sticks with thick globs of hardened sap, eyes were little bits of stone wound into a skeletal head, and from a strangely gaping beak dangled a little, dried worm.

He made himself a sandwich of gamy cured meat and cheese as he sat at the little desk in his room. The whole affair was beginning to become uncomfortably surreal. There had been some hope that beyond the facade, he would have found something comforting that still held some aspect of normal life. Some tether to the real world that would show that, while he was far from the stressors of his everyday, it still existed, was still known here. Though here he sat under a dark cloud, sipping from a bottle of whiskey by the candle that would serve as his only light come nightfall, and hearkened on the way that the wash women had stopped talking when the saw his approach on the walk back, their furrowed brows. He stood by his response to their ridiculous ways of treating that woman, but still felt a bit of a stigma from it.

At dusk he saw a string of people file down the street, and the occupants of the inn joining from the door below. He watched as they all moved slowly and single-mindedly toward the great hall, its front a darkening plane, only illuminated by a pair of points of light rising from the center. Other spots of light moved about toward the hall when the sun finally fell behind the wall of trees in the west, and Joe lit his candle there, in the now dark room.

The windows, which during the day gave no noticeable impact, flickered briefly and burst into brilliant, back-lit life, in the form of a forty-foot-wide hawk, its eyes a dull, grey cloud that gave the slight impression of swirling, churning unlife. Soon, there came a deep and distant rumble that flooded through the window and filled the room—a squealing shriek in response, too high and undulating to have come from human throats. The timber walls rumbled, the branches above the hall swayed, and a hum formed between the shaking floorboards. The rumble grew louder and still the shrieking gained, a bursting steam whistle of sound. He covered his ears, his eyes watering. Tree branches were dragged back toward their trunks as a mountain of wind careened past. There was the sharp grind of a glass pane cracking somewhere nearby, he thought even the moonlight wavered at its source, and, just as the strength began to bleed from his knees, it all suddenly ended. A silent hush, even the more quiet through the hum in his ears, fell over the town, and the tree branches fell into a cadaverous stillness.

Light hymnal music found him, as clear and crisp as if he had been right there. Though even with that clarity, it was in no language that he had ever heard, or anything resembling one. There was a strange bifurcation to the tone and the thump—like that of a helicopter—came in the background, and the light behind the winds flickered, giving the impression that those great glass wings themselves flapped.

The hymn died down, and a faint sermon could be heard. Lost was the clarity that he had heard, just the normal sound of some lengthy, distant rhetoric. Eventually, even that was silenced, and lights could be seen after a short time, dancing in all directions down the streets. A door opened and light glowed between the floorboard slats at his feet. Hush conversations came from below and were constantly checked when their volume neared the point when it could have been understood, and darkened, diminutive eyes stared at him from the bedside table, lit from below with a lace of smoke crashing into its twig and vine beak.

———————

He knocked the empty bottle from his nightstand. His skin felt baked from the light that shone through the window and across his face, and a thick paste of old whiskey and smoke coated the inside of his mouth. He rolled over and pressed his face into the pillow. It didn't matter what time it was—it was too early.

The shouts and laughter from outside rattled in his skull and the smell of roasting meat churned around in his stomach. He stretched the last of the liquor stiffness from his arms, rolled out of bed and put on his shoes. The promise of a fresh set of clothes, clothes that didn't itch and pluck at the hair on his arms, and maybe a cup of coffee, dragged him to the door and down the stairs. At the far end of the hall, a circular window gave view of a glistening lake, fenced by cattail, and the great expanse of pines beyond.

"What can I get ya, Joe?" the bartender asked.

He wasn't going to bring up the events of the night before. It wouldn't be the first time that an alcohol-fueled dream had seemed like reality, and definitely not the first that he had been made a fool because of them. If only he could remember when he had drunk the rest of the bottle. Still, this had seemed much more real than the others. He shook the thoughts away. A group of men were lined at the far end of the bar, sipping from mugs and staring, staring silently at the wall in front of them.

"Um, just my clothes if you get a chance." He glanced over at them from the corner of his eye.

"Sorry about that. Got some rain last night and they're still dryin'." The bartender reached below and pulled out a paper-wrapped package. "I got ya a new set, though."

"I mean, how much—"

"On the house. Looks like a low turnout for the festival this year, so you're damned near the guest of honor."

"At least let me give you—"

"I won't hear of it. We need someone that isn't here for the celebration tonight, so the way I see it, you're doing us a favor."

"I guess."

"And I'll bring your clothes up just as soon as they're ready."

Joe took a seat at the bar. Through the thick layer of shellac, he could feel the grooves of the wood grain. He stole another glance at the end of the bar and couldn't help but feel that their staring at that blank wall was intentional, some statement to him. What the hell could they be looking at?

"Help you with something else, Joe?"

"Oh, I'll just have a whiskey rocks."

A laugh came from the end of the bar.

"Sorry, can't sell any hard stuff on *Fête Faucon.*"

"Fuck." Knowing that he couldn't drink off some of the hangover intensified it that much more.

"Let me get you something that might help." A mug, filled a quarter of the way with some dark brown liquid, was sat before him. The smell of earth and medicine wafted up and bits of leaf and something spongy floated about the bottom. "Trust me, it'll help."

He emptied the mug in one long sip and a bitter sting filled his nostrils, a waxy, oily layer coated the inside of his mouth. Little bloated bits slid across his mouth and stuck in his throat, but he fought it down. His hangover started to recede, to slip beneath the waters of some strange mellow that filled him not like whiskey, but some daydreaming half-sleep.

"Tastes like death, but it'll do the job," the bartender said and left to the back room.

He turned blatantly to the men that now openly looked in his direction, chuckling, the wrinkles of their old faces pulling taut and drooping back into cascades of sagging flesh. The left eye of one was blind—a foggy nebula like the glass hawk from the night before. Unless that had just been some liquored nightmare, he couldn't tell at the moment.

———————————

The street was a chaotic mass of motion and sound, a joyous rush and bustle of roasting sides of meat and hanging summer wreathes—children running by with crowns of brown, striped feathers in their hair and winged crosses pinned to their chests, shouting in the unintelligible chatter of excited youth. Groups of ladies passed by with dresses a little lower, a little more passionate in color, and the slightest hint of blush on their cheeks.

Piles of leaves, fresh and dried, were being burned in stout, wooden barrels, giving off huge plumes of blue-grey smoke. The peak of the summer demanded attention, fighting for those last few breaths before the quick decline of death. Soon it would be hot chocolate and mittened hands, the approach was already felt at night's pinnacle. Joe was guided from the street as a group of men carried past a large birch platform, held together with thick, dried vines and a cart of freshly carved decoys were pulled over to a stand of nearby trees. It was strange business. The sun fell behind a cluster of clouds, and in that slight drop of temperature, he felt the need to walk, to find some quietude.

Laura had loved the late summer, the heat, the sun. He twisted the skin on his wrist until it screamed. He focused on details to batter the ghosts away. Towering wooden torches were being erected at the edge of the woods. The door to the hall stood open, its interior a dismal twilight. In the far corner, the birch platform was being secured to others, like the tight framework of some tall stage or an odd, miniature room. Sitting beside it were two dented copper bowls. After a nudge, one of the workers approached and, without a word, shut the door in his face.

At the center of a small crowd on the side of the road, a man dug the tip of a long blade into the cracked, brown stomach flesh of a whole, roasted pig on a table. Juices poured out of the cut like boiling tears, its mouth pinned open into a perpetual scream, and with a plunge and quick twist of the knife, the gouge split and a pile of apples and potatoes tumbled out. A child squealed and was handed one of the wrinkled pieces of fruit.

As he made his circuit, Joe found himself at the place where he had entered town, the place where that beautiful girl had left. He kept finding himself there. It seemed too quiet, so peaceful just on the other side of those trees. The shine of her eyes, that crimson crescent that was her little smile. He'd just go over for a second to see what was down farther along the path.

Children chanted, grease and sweets smeared across their faces, kites of inverted V's flying high. "Serpent gamin won't know your face, if you dodge the fallen place. So, we let the outside in, and never let it out again. Take it in and lock it up—"

"Don't be going out there."

Joe turned to see one of the old men from the bar was attached to the hand on his chest.

"Excuse me?"

"It's not good to go over there."

"And why in the hell can't I go wherever I want?"

"It makes some of the townsfolk uncomfortable..."

"To go for a walk?" He was feeling ever more like some exhibition.

"Let me buy you a drink instead."

"I think I can do without any more of that shit from this morning."

"None of that crap. Good grain whiskey."

There was a gasp and a child started to wail from behind him. "Alright."

———

"So I gotta ask, what's with all of the birds and shit?" Joe asked as he put down the mug on a table in the inn's dining room. The bartender pretended not to see what they had poured into their coffee.

No one said anything for a few moments, and didn't appear as though they would, until the man with the eye like a blue marble in a glass of milk suddenly slurred, "you'll see the glory of the Grand Faucon at dawn, young outsider!" He cackled while the rest of the faces at the bar shot sternly toward him.

"Shut up, Tom," the bartender said.

"The great benevolence of Faucon shall be imparted on us, his true followers, through the casting out of the impure!"

"Shut your damned mouth!" The bartender smashed down the glass.

Tom's chair fell back as he stood, gave a long scowl around, which locked onto Joe, and stumbled out of the inn. The rest of the men gave one excuse or another to leave shortly after, and, with the whiskey gone, Joe had no reason to remain, either.

"Sorry about Tom. Once they hit a certain age, a man with a drink turns back into a child. Them old myths are given another time as a reality," the bartender said as Joe passed through the door.

His heart beat waves of fire through his temples, the knuckles of his right hand throbbed with the tension of his fist. He was tired of the surreal, tired of some strange set of rules about where he could go, who he could talk to. He'd go where he wanted, when he wanted. Someone said something ignored as he passed through the little patch of trees and onto the path. The false birds judged from above and he wanted to tear them down, smash their heads into little bits of wood.

While he stood there, fuming more than he knew he should be, the girl with the brilliant eyes turned the corner and came into sight. The ends of her long, orange cowl danced in the wind and a basket was slung over her arm. The lilting song that she hummed was carried on the wind to him, and she stopped at each of the holes on the side of the path, reached into her basket, and dropped something in.

"Oh, um, how are you?" he smiled and asked when she was near.

As her eyes dropped to his shirt, her smile vanished, her eyes squeezing to a confused squint, and she turned and ran back down the path.

———————————————

Nearly everything was packed, not that there was much to begin with, the only things remaining being a book and that vile bird. He wanted nothing to do with it. He didn't like the way that the dead eyes stared at him, and wanted nothing to remind him of this time. The afternoon was turning to evening and everything was washed in gold. He had just finished changing into his own clothes, when there was a knock and he opened it to the bartender standing there.

"The clothes didn't fit well enough?" he asked, glancing over Joe's shoulder at the bag.

"They fit fine, but I'm going to get going."

"You're not staying for the feast?"

"I'm afraid not. This place is..." he thought better of finishing that sentence. "I'm just a bit homesick."

"But, how are you going to leave?"

Shit. He had totally forgotten about the car.

"How far is it into town?" Joe asked.

"Just stay for—"

"How far is it?"

"Not far if you know that way. If you don't? You'll never find it."

"Then I'll pay someone to walk me there."

"I don't think you understand how seriously the people of this town take today, Mr. Evans. *Nothing* is going to disrupt the plan."

The tone and new formality struck Joe. "Well..."

"Your car should be ready by the morning. I'll take you myself tomorrow. That is the only option. As for tonight, just enjoy yourself. There's a lot of ceremony, but the food's good."

A pig, painted in orange and black stripes, was tied to a ring, squealing at the front door of the lodge. The ceilings were low, like some subterranean den, and you could tell from the lack of any type of give that the floorboards were incredibly thick. One long table stretched from nearly one end of the massive hall to the other, piled with fruit, vegetables, and cheeses. At the center, an oval sat cleared in preparation. A band played in the corner, some bizarre take on colonial music.

Joe sat at the table, the only person seated, save for a few decrepit men and women, whose heads bobbed on skeletal necks. Eyes were on him whichever way he looked, whispered statements sent from party to party. There was a low rumble, nearly inaudible in its depth but felt through the soles of his feet. A hush briefly fell over the crowd, the musicians stammering a few notes before falling back into line. There he sat silently, for what felt like hours. The bartender had vanished into the crowd, and he recognized anyone else simply in passing, not by name. A silent cue was given, and the partygoers came and filled the bench at either side and across from him.

He watched them eat. Knives slicing into plump flesh, grease-slathered mouths chattering around mounds of chewed potatoes and vegetables. Pots of that fungal tea were passed around and a bitter blend of cranberry and some unknown ingredient. The bodies at either side pressed in tight against him. The band still played at a furious pace, violins screaming, drumsticks a blur. Laughter echoed against the walls, walls that loomed like the edges of some mass coffin. Dust flared in the candle flames. His shaking hand clattered his fork against the plate and a bead of sweat rolled down the back of his neck.

"Welcome guests," a middle-aged man said, as Joe was about to run for the door, and everyone fell silent. "This has not been an easy year for us. We have lost members of our flock both on foot and under the soil. The hands of fate have not always been kind, but we must keep our faith in the infallible overseer, He who protects us at all times, for He is the true glory. He keeps that from below from reaching us. He, and only He, brings the joys that vanquish the hardships!

He waited for the murmuring agreements to die down, and continued, "We nearly failed this year at doing our part for the Grand Faucon, my good family. There is but one condition that he has given to us, good people. One obligation that we have. Our one obligation is to have the outsider to give to Him. Though the world is changing. We cannot always expect the masses to choose from, the groups to choose the fittest from, that I now know. To fail is to show a lack of love for Him, that we are not the chosen followers."

Joe felt the pressure at his sides squeeze tighter as a sad mumble fell over the crowd.

"But succeed we did! Now, no, no, no, do not give me any thanks. It was from the righteousness of you good people, the love that you exude, that the outsider has come. It may have just been one, but what a shining example he is. Even though he may have briefly been tempted, and gone to the place that you do not go, he returned stronger and, yes I'll even say, purer, more perfected by his lapse from the Promised Land! Now before you finish your meals, I want you to thank our gift to Him, Mr. Joe Evans! The drink of life now!"

Sweat-coated hands clapped and fevered eyes stared at him, maddened, rabid eyes that burned with blind zealotry. The plump woman to his left pulled him in tight, and muttered something in his ear, lost in the roar of cheers. At his right, a rough hand pressed down on his shoulder. An ornate cup was pressed into his hand, and he was told to drink, ordered to. From the moment the cup touched his lips, it was pressed back by powerful hands. Moonshine and vegetation and something that told him of a vibrant flower flowed into him, mouthful after mouthful. He choked, but the cup was only tilted back farther. A guttural sloshing crashed into his mind, the last few months a nonlinear swirling of colors, smells, sights. As the empty cup was finally lowered, he felt, but couldn't hear, another deep rumble through the floor.

A haze of moonlit streets and drunken fog occupied his walk back to the inn, stumbling steps swirling and bounding from curb to curb.

"...told you not to let him drink before..." "...get him into the cage?" A colony of bats passed across the moon, dancing into each other for food, and dissolving into a galaxy of black stars that dotted the sky. "You always worry about them breaking out. They never..." Joe looked at his hand, and even with one eye firmly shut, a fan of other hands sprawled across in layers from his own. "...how exactly is he going to be able to stand through the ceremony?"

He opened his eyes, standing in his room, the candle flickering at the table. The contents of his back were strewn around the room, a cigarette burning in one hand, his feet bare. How long had he been standing there? What time was it? The word dawn brushed the back of his thoughts, and the miasmal vacancy poured out of him. He had to go. He stumbled a few steps forward and one back, catching himself on the edge of the desk. Outside, the streets were still pulsing with people, cheering and drinking. He steadied his hand, slid the window slowly up, and dared a glimpse below. A few men stood quietly at the front door, rifles over their shoulders. The edge of the wood was alive with massive, raging torches. Joe recognized the bartender at the center of a larger group that had formed in the street. The group's energy grew more frantic, arms swung about and silent shouts were thrown toward the bartender. A lantern was thrown down, the burning oil sliding across the dirt and a finger was thrust toward his window.

Joe jumped back from the sight, his heartbeat a rattling shiver. He swayed as he threw a few pieces of clothing into a bag when, his head flush with fear and booze, he stumbled into the table. He dropped the bag. The candle rocked, fell, and went out as it hit the ground. There was a fresh shout from outside. Where were his shoes? Where were his damned shoes? The inn door opened, and the floorboards burst with light and muffled argument. He rushed into the hall as quiet steps were heard on the stairs. The fog came over him again and he slapped himself to clear it away. The turn of the stairs grew brighter. He twisted at the locked door across the hall and turned to the end. The circular window of deep-sea blue reflected the light that grew ever brighter at the top of the stairs.

He tugged at the little latch that dragged the window open, quarter-inch by quarter-inch, in the untreated frame. There seemed to be some disagreement going on just before the turn of the stairs, he could hear the consciously-subdued but harsh voices against each other. With one pull, hard enough for the ornate metal to slice through the tips of his fingers, the window slid open. Joe pulled himself through, onto a roof that extended below, and shut the window as tightly as he could without a handle on this side. The lantern light began to illuminate the window pane and he dropped down, his back to the siding.

He could hear them inside, hear their shouts, hear things being tossed about. At one side the street was a rush. The shouts grew louder. He looked to the other side, the steep grade of the roof, the drop into darkness. He slid down. His body picked up speed. He grabbed uselessly at the cedar shingles, splinters slid into his feet and back. Still faster. The moon was a blob just above the trees. And he fell.

His body crashed into the branches of some huge, thorny bush, and there he lay, in his cocoon of pain. His skin felt like one big coating of slices and splinters. Time swayed, he had done something terrible to his ankle, a slice to his eye flared with each blink. Footsteps approached and he held his breath. A gag rose in his throat and he fought to hold it back.

"...need to find him."

"How in the hell am I supposed to know where he went?"

"You spent more time with him than anyone."

The footsteps receded, his breath came out in one burning rush, and a bird chirped in the trees. Dawn. Dawn.

He tumbled into the shallow river, and dragged himself across, the coppery water rushing against his face. The wooden birds had haunted his escape through the darkness, those vile, unblinking eyes in every branch that he looked to, while the sound of frantic voices fell slowly more distant. Then the sun eased over the treetops and he had found himself at the river. On the far side, a steep, clay beach, veined with gnarled tree roots rose up above him.

At the top, he found himself in a landscape like none he had ever seen. The branches of low trees interlaced, bushes grew grey and sickly, the mossy ground pocked with sinkholes from the width of his finger to pits wide enough to swallow him. It was lifeless—no chirps or squeaks or thuds on trees, just a constant *shh* from all around.

He pushed himself along, he knew that he had to run into someone or somewhere. Even in its wildness, homes and small towns spotted the forest. He wondered, as he trudged through the half-light, how far he had gotten from the town. At that pace, it couldn't have been far. He stepped lightly across the spongy soil in a cluster of tight-knit pits, his ankle shivering through pain. The *shh* was louder, more energetic. Ahead the brightness grew. Ahead was clear.

From more than twenty feet away, he could see that glistening sand rose up into a massive clearing, he could feel its warmth, smell its cleanness. Near the far edge, something glimmered in one tree, then two. He fell into some exhausted stupor when, through a cluster of trees by the clearing, he saw a strip of orange fabric pass. He knew that fabric.

"Hey!" he shouted and stumbled through the last of the trees.

He staggered through the sudden brilliance of light, and into the sand. It felt like the soil below his feet were alive. It slipped and shied. The orange cowl and cloak were faced away, bare arms worked at something on the side of the tree.

"Hey, umm..." he said, when a jolt of fire exploded in his leg. He looked down, and his mind couldn't process as a tail slithered back under the soil. When he looked up, she was facing him, the cloak blown open in the growing wind, her naked flesh covered in stripes of black and orange paint. In her hand, dangling from a rope, was a human skull, chunks of shining glass embedded in the eye sockets. He spun his head and in all the trees around him, colored glass glittered in the eyes of hanging skulls. There was another burst of pain and an orange and black snake slithered away and into one of the holes in the ground. He fell back against the embankment and she drew closer, snakes slithering across her feet. Others came forward from the forest, painted, carrying their macabre trophies. He began to crawl back, up the embankment of sand, and the ground rumbled violently. Sand danced up and hovered in the air. His head swam, fat beads of sweat pushed up through his pores, and his legs faded into some memory of feeling. Still, the rumbling grew louder.

The others waited at the edge of the clearing while she came ever closer. His hands pushed into the sand, feeling scaly skin sliding above and below, those two chunks of ember aflame in the skull, as he pushed himself back. His dead legs left two trails slithering up the hill, his heart a thick, sluggish thud. The shadows growing darker, the light more dazzling. His muscles were a sea of convulsion. He needed to go, but the need was becoming confused. He could see that he was high, but the distance became obscure. She was close, and he smelled roses and vanilla wafting up, could vaguely make out the red shards in her eyes. She crouched and ran her fingers across his clammy skin, but he felt nothing. He pushed himself up on some ridge, and suddenly the sand beneath his hands was gone, and he was tumbling.

Rocks bashed his muscle and bones, cracked into his face, leaving a spray and trail of blood in his wake. He slid, gravel and sand a fury until they escaped him and only air surrounded his body. He landed with a crunch of things broken inside, and dragged himself with one elbow, until the strain became too much, little streams of red vomit seeping from his mouth, and he rolled onto his back.

They surrounded him from above at the edge of the quarry: fifty, maybe a hundred. He had to think each breath into life, it was like his body was being slowly swallowed into some void. The walls surrounding him were strewn with a honeycomb of blackened caves at least eight feet high. He could barely hear over the gurgling sounds that his heart made. Loose rocks were shaken down the quarry walls toward his head, the sand became loose beneath his body. The sun crested the lip of the quarry, a stunning flash that brought the sand around to glittering life. Skulls rained down around him, hitting the soft soil with muted thuds. A great cloud of dust and dirt flowed from the caves, washing over him like a wave, and some motion was seen from its billowy innards. He tried to squeeze his eyes shut against the dust, but found that he couldn't. He could only sit and stare, while the dust settled, at the festering, orange and black flesh slithering by through the cave system—coming closer with each pass.

S.T. GIBSON

REVIVAL

SHARDS of sunlight sliced through the trees as Callie sprinted barefoot through the roiling sea of bodies packed into the forest clearing. The men and women of the Clearwater Assembly had gathered with their children under the sugar maples to hear the Sunday sermon. Callie weaved through them all with dust clinging to her hair and a plexiglass box cradled in her arms. She was small for nine, and snapping skirts and flapping hands ushered her out from underfoot as the Reverend's voice filled the thick August air.

"Brothers and sisters, we are a chosen people in an age of iniquity. We have been appointed by the Most High to proclaim the Word of salvation to this wretched world!"

Callie's foot snagged on an exposed root. She chose to skin herself on the dirt rather than let go of the box, and yelped as her kneecaps struck against the earth. Callie hauled herself back up and balanced the box on her lap, cracking the lid so she could peer inside

"Alright, Georgina?" She asked. "Alright, Petunia? Edgar?"

The sleepy tangle of copperheads inside flicked their tails, and Callie smiled. Her grandfather's church owned twelve snakes and she had named every one. They were her friends if she ever had any, and she counted it her special station in life to ensure that they were comfortable and cared for.

"You best not let your granddaddy see you consorting with those serpents, Callie Ann!"

Callie snapped the lid shut and threw her eyes around the clearing. One of the wizened old women of her grandfather's congregation was marching towards her. Callie attempted to find her footing, but the old woman took her tightly by the upper arm and hauled her to her feet. Her rheumy eyes and long white hair did nothing to distinguish her from any of the other venerable deaconesses and prayer warriors who had been members of the church since before Callie was born. Callie had been haunted by their eyes through Sunday school and often heard them whispering her name when she passed the offering plate down the pew.

"Those are the Devil's creatures," The old woman hissed. "And we are called to subdue them, not take up association with them."

Callie Ann twisted in the old woman's grasp.

"I meant no harm by it, ma'am."

"No harm need be meant for harm to come, girl. I see you during service, muttering strange things to yourself. I see."

"Please, ma'am, the Reverend is calling."

The spinster made a derisive noise but turned the girl's arm loose.

Callie's face burned as she continued her trek towards the cedar platform in the middle of the clearing. None of the other holy rollers gave her any trouble, but she could feel their eyes searing into the tops of her shoulders and the crown of her head. Callie pressed her lips together and reminded herself to ignore them. She was used to being stared at.

Callie clambered onto the stage behind the swaying gospel quartet and set the plexiglass box down with a grunt. Her father was waiting for her, wringing his hands and moving his lips in a silent plea for protection. Josiah Clearwater was spindly and tawny-haired, like Callie, but she had her mother's pale eyes. At least her father told her that she did. Callie had been four when her mother died; she couldn't remember much of her. Just the elusive scent of rosewood and the way she always mixed cinnamon and sugar together to sprinkle on top of Sunday waffles.

Callie knelt before the plexiglass box, craning her neck to catch her father's eye. She pressed her hands, clammy from the humidity and excitement, on the lid. Then she tightened up her stomach muscles and called his name as loudly as she could. Even through the din, Josiah heard her. He always heard her, somehow.

Josiah moved toward her as though in a dream, and Callie popped the latch on the plexiglass box and swung the lid wide open. Josiah thrust his arms into the writhing mass of copperheads and took up handfuls of their sleek, muscled bodies. Then he turned to the audience and displayed the contorting serpents looped around his arms.

The congregation exploded.

Callie watched with bright eyes while her father passed the snakes from hand to hand, his face serene as their tails snapped like whips through the muggy air. In these moments, Josiah was the whole sun to her, the stars and magnolia trees and summer cicada song. She knew she would never be allowed the handle serpents during service—she wasn't *clean* enough for that, the Reverend had told her—but in these moments, she could pretend.

"Stop gawking, girl."

Callie jumped. Her grandfather was standing behind her, mopping his brow with a handkerchief. He was thin as a rail and composed entirely of hard angles, from his jutting chin to his knobby knees.

"Keep your eyes on them serpents. If they get loose into the congregation and someone gets bit, that'll be on your head."

The Reverend had been the greatest handler in the state when Josiah was a boy, but once his son had come of age and started displaying an even greater gift for the taming of snakes, the Reverend began testifying that he was being called to cast out infirmities, and that he would take up serpents again as soon as the Spirit ordained.

Callie Ann had never seen her grandfather take up serpents.

"Yes, Reverend," Callie said. She expected him to move past her, to cast his eyes above her head to someone more worthy of his sustained attention. But the Reverend lingered at her side, watching his son with narrowed eyes and a pursed, pensive mouth.

"Lovely sermon, Reverend," Callie said, because that was how she had heard adults speak to him after service.

The Reverend glanced down, and for a moment Callie thought he might speak to her. But he was looking at Edgar, left alone in the box while Petunia and Georgina rode raucous and free on Josiah's forearms.

"The Spirit sure is moving today," Callie tried again.

This time he did look at her, the corners of his mouth pulling tight as though he had tasted something bitter.

"What would you know about the Spirit, girl?"

Ignoring or perhaps not caring enough to register Callie's crestfallen expression, the Reverend waved towards Edgar's box.

"Lock that thing up," He said, and then took to the stage to shout out the altar call while Josiah spun again and again in the rapture of something Callie could taste but never quite name.

━━━━━━━━━━━━

That night, Callie's father fried up green tomatoes to go with his standard Sunday meal of collard greens and pulled pork. Callie was averse to all green foods as well as pork (she considered pigs too sweet-tempered and smart to be eaten) so she focused her appetite on the tomatoes. As she snagged slice after slice of the crunchy fritters from a platter in the middle of her grandfather's table, he spoke.

"Eyes were wanderin' today during the service. It's been happening more and more lately."

"New sermon series, maybe?" Josiah ventured, splashing his pulled pork with spiced vinegar. "Something on the mission of the church, or the call to charity?"

The Reverend shook his head into his glass of sweet tea.

"Folks need clear doctrine: belief, baptism, and salvation," he said. "I don't want to get anything muddled for them. It's hard enough to keep them from sinning like Sodomites at every turn."

Josiah didn't offer any more suggestions, and the soft clink of silverware filled the small house Callie shared with her father and grandfather. She didn't know why her father kept suggesting things like series and mission projects when her grandfather, who made all the decisions, only ever cared about signs and wonders.

They ate in silence a moment more, night breezes curling into the muggy kitchen through the screened back door, then the Reverend continued:

"I know the Miller boy's been running around with one of the townie girls—it's just a matter of catching him and talking some of the Lord's sense into him before a bastard turns up."

Callie's stomach knotted up. There were a word in that sentence that she knew well enough to understand they ought to be avoided in polite dinner conversation.

"Dad, please," Josiah said mildly.

"What?" The Reverend asked, his voice as sharp as every other bit of him. A muscle in Callie's neck tensed so tightly it hurt.

"Not in front of Callie. Please."

"There's no use shielding a child from the way things are. Especially with her upbringing."

Callie's ears were starting to ring with a far-off tinny sound. Soon, she knew, her body would start to feel clammy and numb, as though she was slipping right out of her skin and watching herself from across the table. It was a familiar sensation, one that accompanied Josiah's frequent conflicts with her grandfather, and the subsequent shouting and slamming of doors. It was always hard for Callie to tell who started these fights, but they always seemed particularly bitter when she was in the room.

"Callie, eat your collards," Josiah said. "Everyone can see you're just pushing 'em around your plate."

Callie happily obliged, thrilled that her father had decided not to push the issue further. But then, as she chewed a salty mouthful of greenery, Josiah said,

"There's nothing wrong with Callie's upbringing."

His voice was quiet and made no threats, but Callie heard the challenge in it. She swallowed hard, willing her father to *stop, drop it.*

"When I was her age I didn't have anyone to straighten me out, and I ran buckwild without strong discipline. Lord knows I didn't do a good enough job rearing you, what with your indiscretion with that waitress. I almost lost you to her superstitions, and I blame myself. I don't want to see the same happen to Callie."

"You didn't stand to lose anything," Josiah said, a hard edge on his voice. "You just refused to accept Victoria, or her faith. If you had married us like I asked there would have been no 'indiscretion'."

The Reverend pointed his butter knife at Callie as though providing damning evidence.

"If that girl doesn't get a clear picture of what's right and what's wrong, she'll end up just like her whore mother."

Callie's face burned as though she had been struck, and the pulse roared so loudly in her ears she felt as though she were underwater.

Josiah's mouth screwed up as though he were going to spit something nasty out of it. But after a moment he took a swallow of iced tea and the expression vanished.

"Callie, did you feed the snakes today?"

Her father's voice was so gentle, so dismissive of everything that had just been said, that for a moment it didn't register. Callie blinked.

"Callie Ann, I asked you a question."

"No," She said.

"I've told you before, you don't eat until those snakes do. They're livin' things; they get hungry like you and me. Go on now."

Callie's fingers stayed locked around the edge of her wooden seat. Everything felt disconnected, like time had skipped as easily as one of her grandfather's Gaither Gospel Hour records. Surely she had missed the rattling silverware, the raised voices. Surely her father wouldn't just let something like that go.

"Now, Callie," Josiah said, eyes fixed on his dinner.

Callie got up from the table so quickly the legs of her chair screeched against the linoleum. She didn't look back as she trotted out the kitchen door, letting the screen slam behind her.

The shouting started before she was all the way down the porch steps into the dirt yard.

Scrubbing at her stinging eyes with a grubby hand, Callie traipsed through the dark to the wooden shed at the edge of her grandfather's property. The electrical buzz of the cicadas swelled up around her ears as she retrieved the heavy iron key from the chain around her neck and slotted into the padlock on the shed door.

Inside, the compact earth was cool beneath her bare feet, and the silhouettes of the snake boxes slotted into wooden shelves were dim in the moonshine from a single skylight. The chirrup of crickets had joined the cacophony of night noises. She was sweating, sickly beads that trickled down her back towards the waistband of her secondhand shorts.

"My mama," She whispered vehemently to herself. "Was no...*whore.*"

She grimaced around the obscene vowels of the word. Her father had told her the truth—her mother had been kind as the day was long, and she could skip a rock farther than any boy, and even though she went to a different kind of church than Callie's family, she went every Sunday. Callie wanted to march right back into the house and tell her grandfather that he was a liar and she knew it.

A door slammed in the distance, and Callie jumped.

She hauled a plastic tub of freshly-dead mice off a shelf and began to deposit them by their tails into each snake box, careful not to open the boxes wide enough to encourage escape. It wasn't that Callie was particularly afraid of dealing with wayward snakes; she was certain they wouldn't bite her or wander too far from home. She just wasn't certain they wouldn't take offense to a chance encounter to someone else. That, Callie knew, would mean the end of the church, and the end of her family.

After feeding all twelve of her friends, Callie slid her fingers, limp with trust and habit, into one of the boxes and scooped out Petunia and her baby, Juniper. Callie was of course forbidden from touching the snakes—the Reverend had explained many times that without the Spirit to fill and protect her, she would be bitten and quickly dead. But Callie trusted her snakes more than she trusted her own family, and she knew well enough which snakes were venomous, which ill-tempered, and which ones just bared their teeth for show.

She draped Petunia around her neck like a feather boa and let Juniper coil around her wrist. Then she sat down with a thump on the ground and dwelled on her grandfather's hard mouth, and the way he always looked more through her than at her. She wondered if he had looked at her mother like that when she was still alive, and suddenly Callie's throat was tight with rage. How *dare* he.

Callie lay on her back, welcoming the dim glow of the night sky on her face. The stars filled her eyes with dazzling silver, sending shudders down her spine. Juniper travelled up her arm as Petunia nestled into her tangled hair, and Callie, not for the first time, urged the Ghost to fill her.

She had tried so many times before to open herself up to the holy euphoria that attended so easily on her father and grandfather, but she was never sure if she was doing it right, or what exactly she was supposed to be feeling.

A trio of cottonmouths at her elbow began to grow excited, snapping their tails against the dingy plastic of their box, and Callie slid open their door to allow Burke, Earl, and Jacob to slither towards her across the ground. The familiar weight of her pets crawling over her ankles and pooling on her stomach centered her, made her feel as though she could swallow the whole world if ever it rose up and tried to snap its teeth at her.

Callie dredged her memory for the few words of the illicit enchantment her mother had whispered to her at bedtime, the one her grandfather had rapped Callie's knuckles for when he caught her muttering it over meals. He had called it idolatry, witchcraft even.

"Hail Mary, full of grace. The Lord is with me."

She was misremembering, she was sure, but it seemed like enough. She felt emboldened by her trespass and repeated the spell again, wringing every ounce of meaning from the words.

"Hail Mary, full of grace. Blessed are thee. Now and at the hour of death, the Lord is with me."

For a moment, there was nothing, and Callie thought it was going to be another silent night. Then, she tasted sea salt, though she was miles from water, and she smelled the dusky warmth of rosewood, though none of it grew nearby.

Callie heard her name, more in her head than in her ears, and turned her face towards the sound. As her cheek pressed against the dirt, her eyes found the dark corner of the shed where a wooden box sat most days out of the year. The glint of slitted eyes sparkled prettily out from behind the slats, and as soft secret words began to fall on her like rain, Callie understood.

The snake spoke out of the darkness and Callie closed her eyes and let God's plans unravel all around her.

She understood.

━━━━━━━━━

Once Callie's dinner had gone cold, Josiah ventured outside to locate his daughter. She was sitting in the glow of the porch light on their wooden steps, a green garden snake hanging from her shoulders. Insects filled the warm night air with a velvety buzz while the snake flicked out a pink tongue to taste the salt of the little girl's cheek.

Josiah lowered himself down beside his daughter and gingerly retrieved the snake, plucking it up by the neck and tail.

"I told you not to fool with these creatures," He said, settling the snake down into the sparse grass and watching it slither away. "You're going to get bit one of these days."

"He's just a lil' old garden snake. He said he just wanted to make me feel better."

Josiah shook his head, pulling out crumpled flax papers and an Altoids tin from his breast pocket. He tapped out a ration of sweet tobacco from the tin and began to roll a cigarette.

"Snakes can't talk, Callie."

Callie scrubbed a puffy eye with the back of her hand.

"You shoulda stood up for me."

"I did stand up for you," Josiah said, illuminating Callie's scornful face with a flick of his lighter. "Your grandfather will never lay a hand on you as long as I'm livin', and that's a promise. When I was your age I got beat for every little thing. You should be grateful."

"You're afraid of him."

"Your grandfather's an important man, Callie, and I respect—"

"He pushes everyone around."

"Don't speak ill of your grandfather. He's done us a great kindness, keeping us on like this after your mother got sick. He practically killed the fatted calf when I showed back up with you."

"He's kept us here, all right. We're trapped like rats." Josiah pulled a stern face, but Callie continued before he could reprimand her. "It doesn't matter though. You'll be Reverend before long."

Josiah paused mid-drag, smoke curling from his nostrils.

"What?"

Callie gnawed at her stubby thumbnail, drawing blood from the cuticle. Her father snagged her wrist and dumped her hand in her lap.

"Don't sass me, Callie Ann. I asked you a question."

The little girl rolled her shoulders back and gazed up at the cloud-wreathed stars.

"Well, if grandpa dies, that makes you the Reverend, right? It's gonna happen someday, I figure. I think you'd be a good Reverend. Folks at church think so, too. They say so when they think nobody's listenin'."

Josiah plucked the cigarette from his lips and looked at his daughter hard. Callie refused to meet her father's eyes, just drew coiled shapes in the dirt with her fingers instead.

"Have the snakes been talking to you again?" Josiah asked. His tone was even, but his jaw was tight in the low yellow light.

"Snakes can't talk."

Josiah reached out to brush a bit of grime from his daughter's cheek and sighed. "Go get yourself ready for bed. Revival will be here before you know it, and you're gonna need your rest."

Callie obediently pulled herself to her feet, kissed her father's stubbly cheek, and went back inside the house. Josiah watched her go, smoking deeply and wondering.

━━━━━━━━━━━

The Clearwater Assembly joined forces with the local Holiness Church and Gnatty Branch Signs and Wonders Tabernacle to host a three-day long revival each summer. Like any proper Southern revival, there was old time gospel music, innumerable potluck dishes, and big, beautiful white tents full of ladies fanning themselves with sermon leaflets. Callie always worked the mornings of the revival, sometimes spending as long as four hours ferrying snakes to and from her grandfather's stage. But once the Clearwater service had ended and the snakes were safely stowed in the back of her father's truck, Callie was free to play Cornhole or Red Rover with the other children. She made a point to get baptized each year in the peak of the day's heat, less for the sanctifying nature of the act and more for the refreshing sensation of being dunked in a horse trough of iced water. She usually spent the rest of the afternoon sun-drying and reflecting on God's blessings while gnawing away at a barbeque rib.

However, this year the Reverend had forgone his usual morning service time in the hopes of drawing in a larger crowd at three in the afternoon. Callie has gotten in line for the horse trough of holiness at two-fifteen, unable to take the heat any longer, but had underestimated the amount of people waiting to publicly dedicate themselves to the Lord. She ended up skittering back to her grandfather's platform dripping wet and shamefaced at ten-to-three.

"There you are!" Her father exclaimed. He was dressed handsomely in a pressed powder blue shirt and wore his best belt, the one made of genuine leather. "I told you not to wander off."

"Get to it, girl!" Her grandfather snapped. He was already on stage, guzzling a bottle of water and dressed in red and white checkers.

Callie turned on her heel, picking her way through the crowded green at a sprint. Her white dress slapped wetly against her legs, trailing water down the backs of her knees. Some of the more conservative ladies of the congregation sneered at the sheen of her stomach through the almost-translucent fabric. She pushed the shame away and tried to focus her thoughts. This was a big day. There was no room for fumbling.

Callie used both hands to hoist down her father's truck bed, then tossed back the tarp that shaded the small selection of snakes he had deemed fit for a revival. They snapped to attention in their boxes, eyes following Callie warily. She located Petunia and Edgar immediately. They were her father's favorites, although he would never admit to having any fondness for something like a snake. She stacked another wooden snake crate on top of Edgar and Petenuia's box before ferrying the entire load back to her grandfather's platform.

Josiah was swaying behind the band with his hands pressed to the back of his head. Callie lovingly proffered Edgar and Petunia to his outstretched hands, recognizing the other-worldly gleam in his eyes that silently prompted assistance. Gnatty Branch had lent their fiddler to the small Clearwater worship section, and he sawed away at the strings with furious virtuosity. The sea of bodies crushed up against the platform was twice the size of an average Sunday, and Callie saw plenty of faces alight with the horror of witnessing apostolic wonders for the first time. Josiah, as always, was electric.

The Reverend paced the small corner of the stage where Callie and the snakeboxes sat, rubbing his hands together in a sort of agitation. His granddaughter watched him with unblinking eyes while her heart threatened to burst through her chest.

After a few moments, the Reverend noticed the wooden crate.

"Why did you bring that out here? I didn't ask for it."

"Daddy wanted him," Callie lied, smooth as butter though she couldn't remember telling a deliberate falsehood in her life. "Just in case two weren't enough."

"Stupid boy," The Reverend muttered, half to himself. "He knows better than to...stupid."

On stage, Josiah whirled, head tipped back to the swarm of swallows circling through the sky. A woman in the front row was crying and shaking; one of the members of the Clearwater prayer team was taking her by the elbow, speaking in soothing tones.

"Want me to take him back to the truck?" Callie asked, her voice breaking a bit. She had to ask, she knew. It wouldn't be fair otherwise, and Callie figured God cared an awful lot about fair.

"No, no—leave it."

The Reverend crossed his bony arms, tapping his toes out of rhythm with the music while Josiah swung Petunia, ever the good sport, around his neck. Callie couldn't decide if it was the Holy Ghost or a glimmer of jealousy that shined in her grandfather's eyes as he watched his only son defy death to the screaming adoration of the crowd.

"Fetch one."

"Reverend?"

"Fetch me a serpent, Callie Ann. The Spirit is moving. I must attend to it." When Callie stayed rooted to the spot, he actually deigned to look at her. "Go on to the truck. Hurry now."

"Do you want one from the truck or…it's just that it's closer to…well, I reckon we could—" Callie was stuttering, clumsiness slipping out from behind her teeth to perjure her.

"You've got your momma's contentious spirit and your father's sloth, girl. You make me sick with the shame of you. Fetch me a serpent."

Something hot rose up in Callie's throat and her blood burned with boldness. She heaved the wooden box towards her grandfather with a deliberate grunt. A triangular head lifted drowsily behind the cracks in the slats.

"Take Goliath," Callie said. "He's the biggest. Mean, too. Everybody will be so impressed when you…when the Spirit protects you."

Callie raised up her offering and flipped back the lid. The Reverend seized the water moccasin around the middle and strode on stage to join his son. The congregation convulsed with the sight of such a fortuitous thing, and the fiddle screeched out approval. The wind was picking up, sending and electric tingle across Callie's bare arms as her heart pounded in her chest. Her grandfather's face was shining with sweat, radiating ecstasy as he raised the serpent up towards heaven. Callie squeezed her eyes shut and mumbled a Hail Mary.

Without warning, Goliath whipped around and sank his fangs into Reverend Clearwater's forearm.

The congregation writhed like a thing in pain and flooded up on stage to lay on healing hands. Goliath, fat-bodied and sated with violence, slithered away from the body, eliciting gasps and shrieks from those who darted to clear his path. Callie was almost trampled in the sudden uproar, and scrambled up onto bruised knees as quickly as she could. Josiah, still draped with snakes and half-drunk with holiness, struggled to get near his father without bringing the copperheads too close to any of the congregants.

"No one touch that snake!" Josiah was shouting. "That one's ornery, he wasn't supposed to—I said don't touch it, Josephine! Call your brother, have him bring the tong and hooks…"

Josiah was too busy trying to direct traffic to realize that it was already too late. He didn't even know that the deacon had pronounced his father dead until a murmur of despair rippled through the crowd like a tide.

Somehow, Callie found her father in the fray and clung to his leg, sobbing in grief and relief and other emotions she could not name.

"Callie, don't, the snakes—!"

But Callie embraced her father tight as death, sopping clothes and all, and buried her face in his shirt.

"The Lord is with me," She sobbed. "The Lord is with me."

Petunia leaned over from her perch around Josiah's wrist to bump her broad nose against Callie's cheek, but made no move to bite her. Edgar snapped his tail round her neck amicably.

The girl became dimly aware that people were watching her, and looked up to face them through dripping lashes. All the eyes previously fixed on the Reverend's convulsing body were now glued to Josiah, wreathed in snakes, and his daughter, bramble-haired and safe from snakebites. Callie saw fear in their eyes, but also an awe so big it almost looked like love. It felt as though the very ground had shifted beneath her feet.

Above her head, the sparrows screamed and the wail of ambulance sirens filled the air, but Callie could have sworn she heard church bells.

BIOGRAPHIES

STEPHANIE ELLIS writes short story and novella length dark speculative fiction which has found success in a variety of magazines and anthologies. She is co-editor and contributor to *The Infernal Clock,* a fledgling press which has produced two anthologies to-date. She is also also co-editor of *Trembling With Fear,* HorrorTree.com's online magazine.

She can be found, together with samples of her writing, at stephellis.weebly.com and on twitter at @el_stevie.

S.T. GIBSON is a poet, author, and village witch in training. By day she works for an audiobook publisher, and by night she returns to her home on the outskirts of a small New England town to write speculative stories.

A graduate of the creative writing program at the University of North Carolina at Asheville and the theological studies program at Princeton Seminary, S.T. Gibson is the recipient of the Topp Grillot Award for Poetry and the Olivia Grudger Award for Nonfiction. She is the author of the paranormal novella *Odd Spirits,* and her poetry has been featured in *Wordsdance* magazine. You can connect with her on her website stgibson.com, or on twitter @s_t_gibson.

ERIC J. GUIGNARD is a writer and editor of dark and speculative fiction, operating from the shadowy outskirts of Los Angeles. He's won the Bram Stoker Award, been a finalist for the International Thriller Writers Award, and a multi-nominee of the Pushcart Prize. Outside the glamorous and jet-setting world of indie fiction, he's a technical writer and college professor. Visit Eric at ericjguignard.com, his blog, ericjguignard.blogspot.com, or on Twitter @ericjguignard.

COY HALL lives on the border of West Virginia with his lovely wife and handsome cat, where he's an assistant professor of history and writes stories and novels.

SAM HICKS lives in Deptford, South East London, near the river Thames. She spend her days exchanging sarcasms with the local ducks and eating buttered crumpets.

LINDSAY KING-MILLER's writing has appeared in *Glamour Magazine, Bitch Magazine, Cosmopolitan.com, Vice. com,* and numerous other publications. She lives in Denver with her partner, their daughter, and two very spoiled cats. She is the author of *Ask A Queer Chick* (Plume, 2016).

ROMEY PETITE is recognizable by his wire-rimmed spectacles, pinstripes, and suspenders. He loves reading and writing fairy tales, myths, and magical-realist stories that interweave elements of the sacred and mundane. Originally trained as an illustrator, he graduated from the Center for Cartoon Studies and spent some time self-publishing comics before trying to tell stories that don't require pictures to lean on. His short fiction has been published in *3Elements Review,* Scott Thrower's podcast *Fairy Tales for Unwanted Children, Coffin Bell Journal, Luna Luna Magazine,* and *Moonchild Magazine.* Along with cartoonist Laurel Holden, he is co-author of the illustrated middle-grade reader's novel *Spiderella: The Girl who Spoke to Spiders.* He originally hails from New Orleans and now lives in a sleepy little American town with his partner and their pet corgi.

STEVE TOASE lives in Munich, Germany.

His work has appeared in *Lackington's, Aurealis, Not One Of Us, Hinnom Magazine, Cabinet des Feés* and *Pantheon Magazine* amongst others. In 2014, "Call Out" (first published in Innsmouth Magazine) was reprinted in *The Best Horror Of The Year 6*.

From 2014 he worked with Becky Cherriman and Imove on Haunt, the Saboteur Award shortlisted project inspired by his own teenage experiences, about Harrogate's haunting presence in the lives of people experiencing homelessness in the town.

He also likes old motorbikes and vintage cocktails.

ZACHARY VON HOUSER is a horror author and illustrator originally from the storm-wracked shores of Southern New Jersey. He began self-publishing short stories that were written in smoky bars while avoiding spilling whiskey over everything, and has gone on to win the Nosetouch Press ghost story competition and was published in the first installment of their *Asterisk Anthology* series.

COPYRIGHTS

NOSETOUCH PRESS™

Nosetouch Press is an independent book publisher
tandemly-based in Chicago and Pittsburgh.
We are dedicated to bringing some of today's most
energizing fiction to readers around the world.

Our commitment to classic book design in a digital
environment brings an innovative and authentic approach
to the traditions of literary excellence.

*The Nose Knows™
NOSETOUCHPRESS.COM

Horror | Science Fiction | Fantasy | Mystery | Supernatural

Printed in Great Britain
by Amazon